Holdi

By Eunic

'But seek first His Kingdom and
His righteousness, and all these
things will be added to you as well'

Matthew Chapter 6:33.

This novel is dedicated to Tommy, a gentleman that I met recently, and whose life and faith spoke into my heart.

This novel is based on this man's faith through adversity.

ISBN: 978-1-905787-28-9

Written by Eunice Williams in 2011

Contents

Acknowledgements

I have always dreamed of writing my own book. In some ways I have already achieved this in the writing of many short stories and personal accounts of how the Lord has blessed our family in the past.

Now however, I have written my first novel and I hope to continue to write to bring God glory through my stories.

I would like to thank 'Tommy' for giving me the inspiration to write this fiction story, based on watching him go through his own struggles in this life but having no complaint but he still keeps on praising God.

I would like to thank my friends and family for all their encouragement. I write these stories to bring hope and trust and to encourage ladies everywhere who enjoy reading fiction, to reach out and find just how real God is as we struggle through life at times.
Reading stories like this can change our lives as we step out and trust Him at all times. God is not fiction - He is a reality!

To Richard and Kevin thank you for all your help and advice and to everyone at For The Right Reasons for producing my book.

I give my special thanks to two people who have helped me so much and have been my valued proof-readers. Thank you to Richard Syred and Christine Brown for your time and love given to me in helping me produce this novel. Without you, this novel would not have been written so I thank you for your love and commitment.

Finally a big thank you to my husband David for his constant love and support to me especially for praying for me and seeing me through everything I have been through and for being the first person to read all that I write. Thank you to you all.

If you have been blessed by reading this story or if you want to know more about my faith do please contact me and I would love to share more with you.

Contact: e.williams305@btinternet.com

About The Author

Eunice has been married to David for nearly forty years. They have three grown up children: two daughters and a son. Eunice and her pastor husband have lived and ministered in England, Wales and now Scotland.

Despite significant ill health, Eunice tirelessly shares her passion for the Lord and her heart for hurting people. She encourages others in their faith and reaches out to share the love of Christ with those she meets.

This, Eunice's first novel, is sensitively written and reveals, through the story of two farming families, the author's own abiding love of God and her Spirit filled faith.

Tommy Fearne

Chapter 1. **Tommy.**

With the wind blowing in his face, 16 years old Tommy Fearne was trying his best to battle against the weather as he headed home after a hard day's work on the farm helping his father. He had left school at the age of 14 years and was well used to working on his father's smallholding. Farming, he thought, was what he was called to do! He was so happy.

As he climbed over the brow of the hill he could see the old farmhouse standing in the corner of the yard, with the beech trees swishing and swaying in the gusts of wind which was blowing that evening. The beech trees were to the right of the house and were standing strong and tall, trying to fight off the blasts of wind that were blowing against them.

It was autumn time now and the summer had come and gone by so quickly. The leaves, which were falling off the trees in their rusty red, brown and yellow colours, swirled up and around in the air and were blowing about on the ground in front of him. He continued to walk through them, scrunching them underfoot, making loud crisp noises, and added to the sound of the wind as it whistled around buildings next to the farmhouse. Tommy was so pleased to be entering into the warmth and safety of his home again. But he did so like the different seasons of the year on the farm, even though the autumn winds were so cold!

The kitchen door burst open with a bang as the wind caught it when Tommy opened it and stepped into the kitchen. He quickly shut the door again behind him, and immediately he felt the heat from the Rayburn warming his face, and was so welcoming and inviting.

The kitchen was usually the place where Tommy and his family sat in the evenings, and Tommy loved this room the very best, in the whole of the old farmhouse. It was the family room and it was so cosy and homely!

"Ma, I'm home and I'm so glad to be in and out of that cold wind. It is building up into a strong gale out there and it's taking most of the leaves off the trees with it tonight. The autumn is really here now, so we will have to start preparing for the darker nights and the coming of the winter that is before us," exclaimed Tommy cheerily.

"Come on in and have some nice hot soup to warm you through, our Tommy. Take off your coat and boots and sit yourself down here at the table. Your da will be in soon," said Evie, Tommy's mother.

Tommy washed his hands and he made himself comfortable at the table. He was just about to start eating his soup when his father walked in to join them.

"Evening Da. Can you hear those gales blowing up out there? The wind is getting quite sharp now. Definitely a nip in the air tonight," Tommy spoke up rubbing his hands together.

"Yes son, we will need to pop out in a while and just check that there is no damage done to any of the farm buildings and to see if the animals are all safely tucked up in the warm and in the dry. But first we will enjoy our supper together."

Carter took off his old working boots, washed his hands and walked across to the table to eat.

"Your mother has been working hard preparing such hearty food for us," he said as he turned his head towards his wife and gave her a wink. "So come on lad, let's do it some justice."

Carter took his seat at the head of the table and bowed his head as he asked their heavenly Father to bless the food in front of them. Evie was such a good cook. He thanked God in his heart for her. He began to eat hungrily the parsnip soup and the buttered rolls that were set before him. He hadn't realised just how hungry he really was. His tummy grumbled along menacingly, obviously grateful and in need of the warm food too!

The three of them, Carter, Evie and Tommy completed the Fearne family. As they sat at the table that night, they enjoyed talking and discussing the things that had happened during that day. Beech Farm was their very own farm and was situated in the quiet tiny country village of Maxwell.

Carter and Evie had married when they were young: in their late teens. They had met at a church event in the nearby village of Madison. Carter had grown up in Maxwell where they were now living but Evie had moved to Madison with her parents about six months before they met up. Immediately when they saw each other it was love at first sight!

After a short courtship they were married in the wee church in Madison where all of their friends and neighbours came to wish them the best and to watch the happy couple tie the knot!

That day was a special day – July 21st 1909. The church had been decorated beautifully with so many flowers that it felt like a flower festival. Evie had precious memories of their wedding day. Her heart was very full as she thanked God for all that her marriage meant to both her and to Carter.

They continued to enjoy every day of their married life. Together they worked hard on the farm and in the local church where they had many friends with whom they socialised.

Then amazingly God had answered their prayers for a child when they had their little baby son, Tommy, born to them seven years after their marriage. Tommy was a gift from God to them and they counted their blessings!

Carter and Evie were so proud that day, that day sixteen years ago, when their beautiful baby son was born to them. They had decided to name their son Tommy, after his grandfather, who had died just a few years before their own wee Tommy was born.

Tommy would now carry on the family's name. The name 'Tommy' was special for their adorable baby son, with its spiritual meaning of being 'Divinely Preserved.' After waiting for seven years to have a baby, Carter and Evie recognised that God had indeed had His hand upon this child, and had kept him safe throughout the pregnancy and through his birth. God had faithfully 'preserved his life' and now they had their special gift of a son.

There must be a purpose for him to accomplish in his life here on earth, Evie thought to herself, for God has His plans and His purposes for their Tommy.

As she looked across the table that day she secretly thanked God deep in her heart for all His blessings on their little family. She was so grateful to God for everyone and for everything that they had and were.

Carter and Evie had no more children. But God had blessed them with Tommy. They were not bitter towards God at all that no more children had been born to them, but instead they quietly thanked Him in their hearts for what they did have and that was their own Tommy!

After supper, it was usual to have a time of thanks and prayer to their heavenly Father. This was what was known as the 'Family Altar' in their home every day and in many homes like theirs. Most people in that day came together as a daily ordinance to recognise God as the giver of life and the giver of every good thing. It was important to come and thank Him for their daily bread and for His provision for them in everything.

Both Carter and Evie enjoyed showing and teaching their son that God was their provider and the keeper of all their lives. They wanted Tommy to grow up knowing just how real and how good God is.

Tommy had never known anything different. From being a young boy he knew that God was interested in him. He always enjoyed reading the scriptures, listening to Bible stories and Bible readings and the singing of the Psalms.

From a young age Tommy began to memorise Bible verses and some of the Psalms, so he knew how to say these verses out loud in the fields when he was at work.

Tommy felt near to God when he was outside on the farm working in the fields. Simply, he was recognising God's beautiful handiwork in the splendour of His creation all around him, bringing to God much praise and joy from his own heart. Tommy loved seeing the beautiful mountains and hills before him, with the sun shining down upon them and the majesty of the trees standing tall in all their glory. He watched the baby lambs skipping about the meadows and hearing the ewes bleating out their proud call, watching over their young. '*Lord, our Lord, how majestic is your name in all the earth'*. He recited the Psalm from memory.

'When I consider the heavens, the work of your fingers, the moon and the stars, which YOU have set in place. What is man that you are mindful of him? Lord, that you care for us like this'.

Psalm 8 was a psalm that had always touched Tommy's heart. God had made all this creation - all this beauty - and yet he still cared for every single person on the earth including him. He was just an ordinary farm lad in an ordinary little country village and yet he Tommy knew his God, and this God knew him! How amazing was that!

As Evie looked across at Tommy, her thoughts went back over the last sixteen years that they had been a family. She remembered the days when Tommy was a small baby. She remembered when he gave them his first smile. She remembered when he had first begun to crawl and then later as he began to walk his first step. And she remembered when he started to get into all kinds of mischief!

She thought about the first time on that special evening, when Carter had walked into the kitchen and Tommy had spoken out his first word. 'Da!' he had called out and pointed to his father turning his head round to look at Carter, as he entered the room. That moment had been magical!

From that day on as Tommy grew, he soon picked up many different words and was always chatting away to himself. Sometimes they caught him chattering away at the wonder of a chicken in the yard, or when standing and looking in amazement at the sheep in the meadow, or pointing to the cows in the field. His delight at all the animals was obvious to everyone. He was growing up so quickly.

'My, where had all those years gone to?' Evie thought to herself, with her heart full and overflowing with gratitude.

Tommy was a very polite little boy and as he grew older he enjoyed pleasing his parents and wanting to be useful to anyone who needed help. 'Yes,' Evie thought, God was real in little Tommy's life and for that, she was very grateful. She daily continued to pray believing that whatever the future held, little Tommy (although not so little now) would grow closer to God, and would receive many, many more blessings.

Carter and Tommy came and drew closer to the warmth of the Rayburn, to where Evie had already settled into the armchair after the supper things had been cleared away from the table.

Carter reached up to the shelf and brought down his Bible. They read wonderful words from it, which lifted them up and then Carter prayed and thanked God for the gift of His presence with each of them, throughout that day. He thanked God for being with Evie as she did her work in, and close to, their home. He thanked God for being with himself and Tommy, as they saw to the farm work and to the feeding of the animals outside. Never a day went by without their Family Altar time to God, thanking Him for His constant faithfulness to each of them.

Tommy enjoyed these occasions and it would influence him for the whole of his life. He never forgot God's Word, and in later life, he trusted in the truth of every verse, which would bring him the strength and guidance he would need for every step of his journey. He learnt that nothing would happen to him without God being with him. He knew that to put God first in his life meant that God would never leave him.

Tommy was indeed blessed to have such a wonderful example of trusting God for every situation in life, as he had seen in his parents, Carter and Evie. They were the best parents ever, he thought, and this fact brought him great comfort and joy.

"Right then, Tommy, it doesn't sound as if that wind out there has calmed down at all, does it? So we had better go out and check that things are all in order. Just listen to that wind whistling around the house. Come on then lad; the sooner we go out and do this, the sooner we can come back into the warmth again," Carter said, as he rose from his chair and walked towards the door.

Both the men wrapped up well in their warm coats, hats and Wellingtons to brace themselves against the weather outside.

Tommy followed his father out of the door and crossed over the yard in front of him, checking on the chickens and locking them up for the night. Carter went all around the farm buildings to see that there were no doors hanging on by their hinges, swinging in the wind, or any other pieces of timber or equipment blowing around the yard. Sometimes, things such as buckets and bins could be lifted by the wind and clatter around the area, making an awful din! But tonight everything seemed to be in order even though the wind was so strong. All was well and that was good.

Soon they finished their rounds and they wasted no time in returning inside again into the warmth of their cosy kitchen and to see Evie.

Picking up an armful of logs for the Rayburn, Tommy went back into the kitchen and filled up the log basket which was just inside the kitchen door. They needed to keep warm tonight, that was for sure. This wind could make even their snug kitchen feel a little chilly with the draughts which came from under the door and through the windows, he thought to himself - so let's keep it topped up with logs so that a lovely heat would fill the room!

Beech Farm was a small holding where Carter and Evie had lived since they were married. They kept a few sheep, two goats and some cattle. They had a cow for their own milk supply but mostly they reared beef cattle which were out in the fields for the majority of the year.

The yard was small but when walking through it, one could see the chickens and hens scurrying around freely, pecking away at the grit and the gravel looking for tiny bits of food, and only being locked away at night to keep them safe from the danger of foxes attacking them and killing them. Among them were a few ducks and some geese. The chickens and ducks produced eggs for them and for some of the local neighbours and passersby, who knocked on their door to buy their eggs. Outside their farm was a sign with "Free Range Eggs for Sale" on and "Fresh Vegetables and Home Produce for Sale." This enterprise was Evie's department. She enjoyed serving all those people who came and knocked on the front door, calling for eggs and for fresh vegetables or salads from the garden. She soon acquired regular customers and would often have their packages ready for them on those days of the week when Evie knew they would be calling in. Tegan, her special friend, always wanted fresh eggs on a Thursday. Mr. Walker always called for any fresh produce which would be available on Fridays; and so it went on. She liked to be prepared for all eventualities.

Evie kept the home clean and took pride in what she did. The washing was done weekly and very often when the men came home for meals in the middle of the day, they saw the lines of crisp clean washing blowing in the wind. The house, though not overly big, consisted of several rooms – all of which were kept clean and tidy.

All the food that Evie served on her table had been made by her from the produce which they had grown on their farm; lovely homemade pies, fresh meat that had been roasted, fresh vegetables cooked and served out of their own garden. With their own free range eggs she made beautiful cakes. With the fruit from the orchard she made many different fruit tarts and desserts. Evie made her own bread, and with the milk from the cow she patted and beat the milk into cream, and then made her own butter.

Sometimes Carter would catch a rabbit or a pheasant and Evie would make rabbit stew or pheasant pie! No wonder Carter always gave thanks to God for His daily provisions. His wife was the best cook in the whole of the village.

The large farmhouse kitchen was always full of warmth and love for anyone who called to see them with its Rayburn producing the heat. It was not just the warmth of the cooker but the warmth of the love of God which could be felt here that made any visitors immediately feel welcome to this home at any time of day. Their door was always open to callers.

The Rayburn had a lovely hot oven for all of Evie's cooking. There was an old oak table and chairs in the center of the kitchen. Alongside one wall of the kitchen was a large oak dresser with a wonderful display of willow pattern plates, dishes and a dinner set. This dresser caught the eye of everyone who entered their busy kitchen. No one who called to see them could miss seeing this beautiful display of crockery!

Either side of the Rayburn there were two old, comfortable and well used chairs, where Evie did her evening sewing, darning or reading and where the men folk just relaxed after a hard day's work. The kitchen was so calm and peaceful and a place where they enjoyed their rest at the end of the day.

There were two other rooms downstairs in the old farmhouse. The sitting room was at the front of the house fitted out with comfortable chairs and a couple of bookcases full of well used books of all kinds. In the one corner of the room was an old oak desk, full of papers and bills and stationery. One or two plants were on the window sills, bringing a little colour into the room. There were a couple of oil lamps on the small table by the side of the desk for display purposes only now, as Evie had recently acquired an electric table lamp for reading. It hadn't been very long since the electric had been put into the farmhouse, but this was indeed a real luxury for them. Electric light! My, how she gave thanks to God for this gift, as she enjoyed reading so much. The extra light would allow her to read for much longer in the evenings now and would aid her with her sewing and with the mending of Carter's and Tommy's many socks!

The other room downstairs was where Evie kept her food cool and fresh. There was a stone slab where the food was kept covered and cool. With no refrigerator yet in the house the milk was kept cool in the nearby stream where it was put into a container in the cold, slow running water.

Likewise, Carter had made a 'food safe' for the baking to be kept in away from the flies and dust. This area served as a kind of pantry and Carter had made shelves for the different jars and containers of all the food Evie would preserve throughout the year.

This room was kept very clean and tidy, and in order.

Evie was a very ordered person who did things well. She aimed to keep her whole life ordered and strived to reach this, in every part of her daily life so that everything had its place in the old farmhouse.

The stairway went up from a small hallway near the front entrance into the farmhouse. The family rarely used this entrance always preferring to come to the back kitchen instead. Evie was very used to her callers knocking on their front door seeking fresh eggs or supplies of any homegrown vegetables.

Upstairs was Carter and Evie's bedroom in which there was a large double bed and a low dressing table. It also held a sizeable brown double wardrobe which they both shared for their clothes. The farmhouse was quite an old building, so it had a lovely old fireplace in their room which Evie kept clean and fresh looking. This fire was not used on a regular basis but if either of them was ill or if it was extremely cold they would light the fire for more warmth and comfort.

Going on across the landing were two smaller bedrooms. On the right was Tommy's room with his bed, a bookcase, one wardrobe, and a few old corgi cars and lorries stacked neatly in one corner. His clothes and his best shoes were stored away in his very own wardrobe.

To the left of the landing was another room with a single bed in it. This room was only used when they had visitors come to stay. On the dressing table by the window, was placed a blue willow pattern bowl and pitcher for washing purposes, with a neat brush, comb and mirror set, placed by the side of it.

The toilet at Beech Farm was outside the kitchen door, a little way down the path. It wasn't many years after they moved in, that an extension was added to the farmhouse to bring the toilet nearer to the house.

For a while, having a bath was in a galvanised tin tub which was brought in from out of the backyard on a Saturday night and put in front of the open fire. Now though, having the Rayburn made all the difference for them and the whole room was warm and cosy for their bath nights.

Oh, how it felt good to wash away the dirt and grime and to be clean and fresh for the following Sabbath day.

Outside in the yard were a couple of small outbuildings for the animals, with a granary for the harvesting and storing of the grain. The yard had a medium sized barn full of bales of hay and straw. They owned some small pieces of farm equipment, which was not really very much, but they did have a plough, a mangle, a trailer and a few other bits of machinery which was stored in one corner of the barn. The old mangle for chopping up and slicing the swedes and turnips for stock feed, was in the centre of the old barn, handy to get to each day, especially in the winter, when the animals would need the extra food to keep them strong and warm in the bitter weather.

A small chicken coop was built for the chickens to be safely put in at night and where the eggs could easily be collected each day.

Carter was a keen gardener and he had taught Tommy to garden and take pride in his work. Both of them worked hard and as a consequence they were blessed with large crops of potatoes, onions, beetroot, peas, swedes, carrots and salads each year.

Farming and keeping a small holding was hard manual labour and could be very exhausting, but it was also very rewarding and healthy for them.

Carter, Evie and Tommy enjoyed great health for most of the time. They wouldn't live anywhere else! How they loved their life working together in the countryside.

Tommy was very much like his father. He had a strong body and well worked hands. Tommy was dark haired and very 'bonny' looking. He had handsome features that immediately drew you to him, all of which he had inherited from his father.

Tommy's eyes were full of love and laughter and were as brown as his father's and his grandfather's before him.

Similarly, Carter's fine looks, with his bright striking eyes, immediately attracted you to take notice of him. Those deep brown eyes were a family trait and oh so beautiful.

Both of the men were equal in height, although Tommy was still only sixteen years old. Both father and son were nearly six feet tall and of slender build. In fact, when they were out together, from a distance, it would be quite easy to have mistaken one for the other. Tommy, who looked so much like his father, also grew to be like him in nature as well and would help anyone out in time of need. Both of the men were highly respected in the community where they lived, for they showed the love of God to their entire neighbourhood.

Many of the local farmers would help each other out at busy times, such as in the springtime when the lambing season was in, or in the summertime during haymaking time, or in the winter when animals were put into buildings to shelter from the cold weather and when more feeding would be required.

This community, the tiny village of Maxwell was a close community and the inhabitants saw to it that nobody was left without help at any time.

There were many of the neighbouring farms surrounding Beech Farm and all close enough to be of support to each other.
Further along again, were many terraced cottages leading into Maxwell a small village which consisted of a general store, a post office and a church.

About a mile or so further on along the road there was also a wee village school, Maxwell Primary. The children from the surrounding area all walked to school together and home again in the late afternoons, enjoying skipping around and kicking up the leaves in the autumn months.

Heading in the opposite direction were more farms. Carter and Evie had some special friends who lived along this road. They met up as often as they could especially when the children were younger when they would play together in the evenings. They were very close friends.

Another family, the Norman family, lived just a mile away from them at Gooseberry Farm, turning left at the top of the hill which was just on through the village. Carter and Malachi Norman had worked alongside each other in all the busy seasons over many previous years. They were of a similar age with Malachi being a little older by five years. Working together in the same occupations they would share workloads and help each other out, especially at busy times of the year when days were long and exhausting.

Malachi and his wife, Tegan, along with their two daughters, Peggy and Patience, became firm friends with the Fearne family, especially now as it seemed that Malachi was finding it very difficult to do his work these days. His body seemed to be refusing to do what he wanted it to do and Malachi was so concerned that he couldn't seem to accomplish anything to his own satisfaction. Carter did his best to encourage him and support him, but over the past couple of years he'd noticed that Malachi had been struggling to do the physical work, and he watched as he saw him struggling within himself just to keep on going.

Each Sunday throughout the year, Carter, Evie and Tommy would walk along the road to worship in the local church. Malachi, Tegan, Peggy and Patience also went to this church, as did many other of the locals from their village. The vicar, Rev. Malcolm Lovell, was a welcoming person and his congregation loved him very much. The church congregation was a very kind and very caring group of people, who looked forward to church on Sundays. They sang out heartily to the God who had continually provided for them, year after year and for each day of their lives.

All the children had gathered together, including Tommy and the Norman girls, for Sunday school classes and worship. Sunday school had been interesting as the children had been taught to learn and memorise scripture verses and sing wonderful songs and hymns together.

Because of the 'Family Altar times' in their individual homes and being able to see the beauty of the countryside around them, these children all grew up to know that God was the Creator of the world. This God who had created all this beauty was indeed awesome! They did not question this fact: the fact that God was real - for they knew it in their hearts! They could see the evidence in front of their own eyes so they enjoyed worshipping Him in the songs they knew.

Tommy and Peggy, along with the other children, often enjoyed walking through the country lanes, watching the birds, or viewing the landscapes in front of them. Everything just revealed the majesty of God. The wonder of a large oak tree! The beauty of a sunset! The brightness of a beautiful rainbow in the sky which God placed there after the rain showers, reminded them yet again, that He was alive and in control of the whole of creation; the trees, as they shed their leaves in autumn, the glistening of the snow on bitterly cold winter mornings, the beauty of the snowdrops in the spring and the sweet fragrance of the roses in the summertime.

Often, on their way to and from church on Sundays, the children had sung from their hearts, the words of the hymn that seemed to be their favourite, *'All things bright and beautiful'* being amazed with the words as it exclaims, *'The Lord God made them all'!*

One of their favourite verses was from the book of Genesis, *'And God saw all that He had made, and it was very good.'*

They so loved this God who revealed Himself to them every day through His Creation. Their lives were happy and joyful.

Chapter 2. **The Norman Family**

Peggy and Patience were a great help to their parents and had been so excited when Tommy and his dad Carter joined them on the farm for days of harvesting and for the ploughing of the fields. The children had all grown up together and played as brothers and sisters. They had shared all of their secrets and had enjoyed being together in all their escapades; climbing trees, hiding in the meadows and picking fruit in the autumn off the trees and bushes. They also remembered games of 'Hide and Seek' and 'Tag' which they had played when they were younger.

Sometimes Peggy would call at Beech Farm to buy some eggs from Evie for her mother. They did not have chickens on Gooseberry Farm so she enjoyed going across to fetch the eggs. At these times when he was not too busy helping his father, when she was leaving to go home again, Tommy would walk part of the way home with her. Tommy enjoyed Gooseberry Farm and was as fond of it as he was of his own farm.

On this particular day, Tommy was just pottering about in the yard, when he heard Peggy's voice, calling out to him.

"Hello Tommy, what are you up to today? I have come to see your Ma, to see if there are any spare eggs for us. May I go in and see her?" enquired Peggy.

"Aye lass, you are very welcome to go in. Ma is in the pantry. Just let yourself in and give her a call. She will hear you. I will see you in a wee while."

"Mrs. Fearne! Mrs. Fearne! It's Peggy here. Do you have any eggs we can have please, for my Ma is going to do some baking today?" Peggy called out, as she opened the kitchen door, and let herself in.

"Hello lass, I will be with you in a minute," Evie answered her, "Just sit yourself down and I will get the eggs for you. One dozen is it?"

"Yes please, Mrs. Fearne, thank you," Peggy replied.

As Peggy looked around her she was so happy. She loved being in this home. Tommy was so lucky to have such a lovely house and such lovely parents. She noticed the pretty willow pattern plates on the dresser, and got up to go and see the wonderful display that was in front of her. She was always drawn to this lovely array of crockery on their dresser. Actually, as soon as you stepped into this kitchen, you could not help but notice this display, she thought to herself! There were so many patterned plates of all shapes and sizes, lined up on the shelves along with other dishes and vases all of the same design, that it simply amazed her! It must have taken ages to have been able to afford all these plates and dishes, she thought to herself. I wonder how long Mrs. Fearne has been collecting them. She could not remember a day that she had come into this kitchen, without noticing this amazing dresser.

She was so engrossed in looking at one of the vases that she now held in her hands, that she didn't even hear Evie when she came back into the kitchen.

"Why lass, you are always taken up with those dishes and things, aren't you. One day you will have some plates and dishes of your own, and when you do, I will give you a plate off my dresser for you to treasure. How would you like that lassie?" Evie asked her.

"Why, thank you Mrs. Fearne. Can I r-e-a-l-l-y have one of your plates?" exclaimed Peggy with delight.

"Of course, my dear, you can choose one off the shelf right now, and I will keep it safe for you, I promise," Evie answered her, "and when you marry, I shall give it to you for you to have in your very first home."

"Thank you, thank you, thank you so much, Mrs. Fearne," she squealed with delight, as she reached up and chose a tiny oval shaped plate. Touching it and holding it, she pointed it out to Evie. "This one please, this one, I would love to have this one, if I may. It's quite a different shape from all the other plates here and to think it will belong to me one day!" Peggy exclaimed.

"Then I shall mark it for you and put your name on the back of it and one day it will indeed belong to you Peggy dear. Now, sit down and have your drink."

A little later on, Evie said to her, "Now you away home lass and take your Ma these eggs. God bless you. I will see you next week."

Peggy turned to go out of the kitchen door just as Tommy was making his way inside.

"Come on then, Peggy, I will walk with you some of the way home. I see you have your eggs then. Mind you don't break any of them. Come on away then. I will be back soon Ma. I won't be long," he called out to Evie as he shut the kitchen door behind him.

They hadn't gone very far down the road when Peggy told him about the plate that his Mother had put aside for her.

"Tommy, I can have one of those plates off your Ma's dresser, as my very own one day. Your Ma said I can. I can't wait to have my own house. Do you think I will have such a great display as your Ma has on her dresser one day, Tommy? It's so wonderful. I would love to have one of those for myself?" She pondered a little, "I wonder where I shall live and who I shall marry when I'm older?" she asked, as she looked up at him enquiringly.

"Why of course, you will marry me, Peggy Norman," he said astonished! "Wouldn't you like to marry me? Anyway, who else would you marry?" he teased her. "We will always be together Peg, forever!"

"Aw Tommy, we are just mates. We've been friends forever. Of course I like you and I would love to marry you, but I think that some young man will come into my life one day and just sweep me off my feet," she said romantically!

With that Tommy burst out laughing and lifted her up and ran along the road with Peggy waving her arms about and kicking her legs in the air shouting, "Put me down, our Tommy, are you soft in the head? Put me down!" she said giggling merrily!

Tommy put her down gently so as not to break the eggs and then watched as Peggy walked home the rest of the way up the hill with such joy and happiness in her heart. They gave each other a quick wave and separated happily.

Tommy went back home to the farm to see his mother, thinking about what he and Peggy had just been talking about. Somehow, he felt a little disappointed deep down inside him. *Would* he marry Peggy one day or would she just go off with some person who would come along and sweep her off her feet as she had said? He realised now that he felt a little sad at the prospect. Peggy was his special friend. She belonged to him. She was his!

Chapter 3. **Trouble**

Two years passed and another Sunday came around. As was customary the Fearnes and the Normans met up in church. They sat in their usual seats in the church waiting for the service to begin. Other people were arriving and just as it was time to start the service, the church bells rang out at 11.00am for the whole village to hear and be reminded that once again it was the Sabbath day. The minister stood up and announced the first hymn. Everyone sang out their worship to the God who had been faithful to them through yet another week.

A little way into the service the younger children in the congregation filed out to Sunday school. Tommy and Peggy, now eighteen years old, stayed in their seats to enjoy the whole of the service. They both sat back to listen to Rev. Malcolm Lovell as he preached the sermon for that day. They wanted to hear from God.

The text that morning was from Matthew chapter 6: verse 33. *'Seek ye first the kingdom of God and all these things shall be added unto you.'*

Tommy listened attentively to the message. As he did, he realised again just how much God loved him and how much God wanted him, Tommy, to love Him in return with all of his heart.

When Tommy left church that day, he held onto that text in his mind and thought about what it meant. *'I will* seek God and put Him first in all of my life,' he thought to himself. He remembered Rev. Malcolm speaking about how much God cares for people, for everyone, even him.

'Why should I worry about things, when God says He cares even for the birds of the air? He feeds them and looks after them all of the time. They don't have to worry, for they know that God will take care of them. I will always remember that God wants me to never forget Him, and to know that He always knows all about me and cares for me. He will guide my life, my whole life, when I put Him first. I will 'Seek God First' and then I will know His blessing and His constant care for me.'

This text became Tommy's lifeline for the remainder of his life. God WAS FIRST in all he thought and in all he did, from that day on. He had decided that living for Jesus, was so very important.

With the service ended, Malachi and Carter were walking out

together when Malachi asked his friend if it would be all right to meet up with him soon. He wanted to talk to him about something that he had on his mind.

"Carter, I do need some advice and I need your help. Are you able to give me a few minutes to talk please?" he asked his friend expectantly.

Immediately Carter felt a heaviness and an urgency in his heart. He knew that his friend had been suffering in some way. He had known it really for quite some time, but he didn't know really how much he was suffering and what it was all about. .

"I could call up tonight after the feeding if you like, Malachi. How about 7pm? Would that be convenient for you?" Carter enquired.

"Thank you that would be good. I will see you then. I do appreciate it Carter. Thank you so much," Malachi responded gratefully.

Sitting at the dinner table a little later on and enjoying a cup of tea together after their Sunday lunch, Carter told Evie about his conversation with Malachi earlier on that morning as they were coming out of church.

"Malachi would like me to pop up to Gooseberry Farm to see him later, Evie. I think there is something that's troubling him. I have noticed that he has been out of sorts these last few months, well maybe longer if the truth were known. But I did think and hope that I was just imagining things. I wonder what is troubling him? Has Tegan said anything to you about what the problem might be?" he enquired of her.

"Well actually, she did say something to me a few months ago. She has been noticing that Malachi has been forgetting things and that he has been a bit restless and fidgety of late. She is worried about him, Carter. She asked me to pray for him but not to tell anyone in case she was just being over anxious. Maybe this is the right time for you to talk to him. You go and see how you can help him and I will clear the dishes away."

"Maybe I will go up about 7pm a little later on, when it will be a bit quieter for him. Maybe then, we will be able to have some time to ourselves. Let's pray for God to help him share with me what is on his heart and what is worrying him Evie." They bowed their heads in prayer together for their very dear friend.

The appointed time arrived and Carter knocked on his friend's door. Malachi invited him into the lounge where they would be on their own. Tegan and the girls were busy outside in one of the outhouses locking up the animals for the night.

"Thank you for coming over Carter. I need to be able to speak with someone that I can trust. I do thank you, Carter, very much," he said gratefully and simply.

Carter found a comfortable seat near the open fire and sat down quietly waiting for Malachi to begin.

After a few minutes Malachi spoke what was on his heart. "For the last few years, I have not been well at all. At first I thought I was imagining things. I was forgetting the simplest of things - things I should have easily remembered. Forgetting things I had done yesterday, as well as last week. Then I started dropping items and finding it more difficult to carry objects. I have persevered or I have tried to, Carter. But the more I have tried to do things properly, the more of a mess I have made of them. Sometimes I haven't even been able to say what I have really wanted to say, stumbling over my words. Some mornings I feel I am unable to do any work. I'm so stiff and awkward that I can't even pick up the things that I have dropped. I don't know what's wrong with me Carter, I really don't.

The doctor has not confirmed anything yet but I am obviously not well Carter. I don't know what to do anymore. I haven't spoken with Tegan yet, but I know that she has noticed my moods and my irritableness. I have tried not to cause her any worry and have just passed things off as a joke or me being clumsy. But I know she is worried about me." He hesitated a little more,

"Now is the right time for me to speak with you, Carter. I need your help. I can't keep struggling to hide it anymore." he said, breaking down a little, "It's all too much for me to keep going as if there is nothing wrong."

Carter remained quiet for a wee while longer. Then he held his dear friends' hands and prayed silently with him and for him. They both felt God's presence surrounding them.

But this is far worse than I ever imagined, he thought to himself. How can I help him Lord? Please give me the words to say to him?

After the prayer, Carter responded in a quiet voice full of compassion for his friend,

"Thank you, Malachi, for sharing with me. I am so sorry for your troubles and I'm sorry to see how distressed you are. I have realised myself that you have not been yourself for a little while now. As we have just prayed together, I will continue to ask God to strengthen you and to bring you healing; healing in your mind, so that you don't struggle to try to work out what's wrong physically, and panic even more. I will also pray that God will quieten you in your heart, so that you can trust Him with the outcome. He knows all about you and He cares for you!"

They both sat quietly feeling God's peace filling their hearts again. After a while Carter spoke again, "I can send our Tommy to do your work on the farm for a while, Malachi. Don't worry about that anymore. Tommy would love to come over and help you out. He is a good lad. When he comes here, you just tell him what he has to do, and let him help you. I know he enjoys coming to Gooseberry Farm.

I do think you should try and tell Tegan now though. You both have Evie's and my support to help you through all of this. Evie and I will come over tomorrow and you can explain to Tegan and then she will have Evie here, to share and pray with her after. Tegan does need to know now. You will feel better then and you won't have to strive or struggle anymore in front of her. She will be a help to you and strength for you in all of this. She would want to know, Malachi.

But for now we hold onto God, who is OUR strength and is SO faithful knowing that HE will bring you through this."

"I am now in my late forties Carter. I have been struggling with this for a few years, noticing a little tremor first, followed by my being awkward and clumsy. Now I am jerking more often and feeling unsteady on my feet, so I'm beginning to lose my balance. But I do believe God can heal me. I have been asking Him to do this and I am trying to trust Him with my life each day," Malachi said, beginning to feel a little more hope.

Carter went home and told Evie all about what Malachi had told him that night. They knelt in prayer together and decided to tell Tommy all about it the next morning trusting him with the news, and also asking him if he would go up to Gooseberry Farm to help and work with Malachi.

Thankfully at this time of the year, farm life was not too busy so Carter was sure that between them, they would manage to keep the both farms running smoothly. They would do all they could to help out their very dear friend.

Evie and Carter went to the house the next day and Evie was able to sit down and pray with Tegan and help her to come to terms with the shock of it all, telling her to try and hold onto God. Staying by her side and silently praying, she was a big help and strength to Tegan.

As the months went by, Tommy spent most of his time at Gooseberry Farm. He prayed hard for Malachi as he watched him trying to do what he could, but was gradually deteriorating. It was hard for them all just watching him struggle on.

As Tommy was finishing work at the end of the day, Peggy would come out to the farm building and ask him lots of questions. Sometimes she would cry quietly, and he would just sit by her side and let her share her brokenness and her sadness with him. She was hurting so much watching her dad suffer like this.

Rev. Malcolm called each week to visit and pray with Malachi and Tegan - he always helped to lift their spirits. Rev. Malcolm would read passages from the Bible to bring them some comfort. This was their hope. It was Malachi's only hope; hope in the God whom he had trusted in, for all of his life. The words of the Bible gave Malachi such inner strength, but his body was frail and getting much weaker. Now he was not able to communicate much at all, but he could understand every word that was spoken and what Rev. Malcolm was saying to him.

"Why does God not heal my da, Tommy, I don't understand anymore?" Peggy questioned Tommy, a few weeks later.

"I don't know lass, but I do know that your da trusts in God, and that is good. Whatever happens when you put God first, He will never let you down. He will come to your da in a different way to what we can understand right now. God has not left your da on his own, Peggy. His life is safe with God, of that we can be sure," Tommy said, as he comforted her with his gentleness and kindness.

She could always rely on Tommy to help her to feel better and help her to seek God's help in everything that troubled her. Thank you God for Tommy she prayed silently! I couldn't do this on my own.

Tommy never showed Peggy his own fear - he kept that to himself. He feared that Malachi Norman was not going to get better in this life, but he could see that God would soon relieve him of all his suffering. Tommy was sure that soon Peggy's father would die and go to heaven. But he didn't want to show Peggy that just yet. She would know soon enough, and then he would be there to comfort her and be of help to her. For now, he needed to show her where her strength would come from, for she would need God soon, in a way she had never needed Him before.

Tommy remembered that night a few weeks ago when at the Family Altar, his father had read from the book of John and chapter14, about Jesus preparing a mansion in heaven for those who belonged to Him and for those who are His children. It said that where Jesus was, we would be with Him too if we belonged to Him. He knew deep in his heart that Peggy's father was going to that mansion in the sky that Jesus was preparing for Malachi even now.

Not long after this, the moment came when Malachi was not well at all, in fact, he became progressively worse. He had become so weak that he now needed to be in bed for most of the time, and have as much caring and looking after as possible. Very sadly, Malachi caught pneumonia and weakened even more. Carter and Evie went to the house to stay and help Tegan and the girls, both by their caring and being there for the family.

Everything was quiet in the home the next day, as Tegan knew in her heart that it would not be long now. Soon after, Malachi breathed his last and entered into heaven. His loving wife and daughters were by his bedside as they watched their loved one leave this world for a much better place.

Rev. Malcolm came and prayed with the rest of the family and left them to mourn in peace.

Carter and Evie stayed for the rest of the night while Tegan and the girls tried to come to terms with their loss, and yet they knew they had total confidence that Malachi was with his Lord and Saviour in heaven.

He had had faith and now he was with his God, out of all his suffering. And yet they missed him already! They would always miss him, they knew that.

Tommy sat with his arm around Peggy. They sat quietly together. He knew without a doubt that God would give him Peggy to be his wife one day in the very near future; but he kept these thoughts to himself for now.

Tommy would tell her when the time was right. It just felt so right to be there at her side and bring her some comfort when she was missing her father so much. He also knew that Malachi had seen this too and was pleased that he had had Malachi's blessing to marry his daughter one day!

Everyone was so kind to the Norman family. The whole congregation helped them and some of the church people baked cakes for them as they called with their condolences, demonstrating their love to the family by their visits. Tegan and the girls were surrounded by the love of the church family. They didn't feel alone.

The day of the funeral came and God gave them such a dry, beautiful crisp, sunny day. The church was full of people and all of their friends. Rev. Malcolm gave a powerful message as he spoke about having the assurance of life after death - with Jesus. If you belonged to Him in this life, you would belong to Him in the next. Or the alternative would be an eternal life that would be an eternal life without God and be separate from Him forever.

Malachi died aged 49years. Now he had all of eternity to live a full life in heaven; life for him was just beginning!

Chapter 4. **Moving on....**

It had been about a year now since Malachi Norman had passed away and Tommy was still keeping Gooseberry Farm running for Tegan. Tegan, Peggy and Patience did all they could to help him each day. It continued to be hard to think that they would not see Malachi working on this farm again. How they missed him. But everything was going well and things were getting done.

Tegan knew that it would get more and more difficult to keep the farm running as time went on, so she made enquiries about one of the terraced cottages that was empty in the village. She didn't tell anyone about it but just prayed that God would guide her in this. She had thought long and hard about it over the past couple of months. Yes, she thought, I feel it's time to move on!

When she had everything sorted out in her mind she decided to call at Beech Farm to see Evie and Carter, to share with them the plans that were on her heart. She knew they would help her with all the necessary arrangements.

As she knocked on their kitchen door she heard Evie call out to her, "Hi Tegan, come on in. The door is on the latch." She stepped into the kitchen and saw that Evie was standing by the Rayburn, stirring the stew that was cooking on the top of it. What a delightful smell filled the room she thought and then she realised just how hungry she was.

"That smells so beautiful Evie. And the warmth of the fire is so inviting," she commented, as she sat herself down in one of the cosy chairs by the side of the Rayburn.

"I have something to tell you Evie, but I would like Carter to be here when I say it. I've got something on my mind that I would like to discuss with you both. Will he be home soon do you think? I don't want to take him away from his work though," she said, apologetically.

"Oh that's all right Tegan. Carter will be in at 4 o' clock for a cup of tea. In the meantime, shall we have a drink ourselves?" Evie asked her, as she poured the hot boiling water into the already warmed teapot, sitting and waiting on top of the Rayburn.

"I had been trying to think of a good excuse for a cuppa myself anyway, so it will be good to have a sit down for a few minutes with you."

Tegan thought to herself, I always have such a warm welcome when I come into this home. What lovely friends I have. Thank you Lord for Evie and Carter. Yes, she did count her blessings, although her heart was still sad when she thought of her loss, the loss of her husband and her best friend Malachi. But God had indeed given her these two lovely special friends who meant everything to her. 'Thank you Lord. I am grateful for your care for me,' she whispered in her heart.

It wasn't long until Carter entered the room and joined them both. They all sat together, around the Rayburn in the quiet peace and in the warmth of their comfortable surroundings.

Tegan began to unfold all that was on her heart. She spoke to them, about how much she missed Malachi, her husband and her companion. She spoke about all the suffering that he had gone through over the last few years. She told them how her heart rejoiced when she thought of Malachi now, who was with his Lord and Saviour, free from all pain, with his body healed and rejoicing with Jesus. But oh she missed him so much!

Tegan told them about how grateful and thankful she was for them both, her very dear friends, who had gone out of their way to help her and stand by her so that she could be strong.

All was quiet for a little while. Carter and Evie waited calmly, knowing there was more to come.

"I have been thinking much over these past few months. I love living at Gooseberry Farm and I have been so happy and grateful for all that your Tommy has done, and is doing for the girls and for me. He is such a strength to us all, especially to our Peggy. I see them chatting together sometimes and I feel their closeness. I am glad that our Peg has him to talk to and to confide in.

I sit in the evenings on my own and I think about all the good times Malachi and I have had at Gooseberry Farm over these past years. I think of all the times of blessings with our girls and with our friends there and the many special occasions of just being together. I feel his presence still near to me you know, and I hear his voice in my heart. I know what he would have thought about the things that we do, or have done on the farm over this last year. The farm seems so full of him. It's only to be expected I know....

But I feel it is now time for me to move on... "

Carter was about to say something to her but she said, "Oh

no! Please listen to me Carter. Please let me finish," and kept on speaking, all the while looking at him.

"The house is too big for the three of us now. It will take a lot of money to upkeep it for soon there is work needed to be done on the building. The farm needs someone else to have it as their own, building it up and making it a thriving, working farm for them; someone who will make it their very own. It is now the right time for me to do this, to move on and hand it over to someone else.

I have prayed about it and I have been to see one of the terraced cottages in the village that is empty. It's at the end of the terrace next to Mrs. Grayson. It is available for me to move into next month, if I wish to do so."

She hesitated a little. "I came to see you both, to see what you think, before I complete the purchase. But I have not chosen to do this without much thought and prayer. What do you think Carter, Evie?" she asked of them, "Do you think I am right in this?"

Carter had suspected that this was what Tegan was about to say, so he answered her slowly,

"Thank you Tegan for coming and telling us about the plans you have. As you have been speaking I have felt the same peace in my heart. I think you are making a wise move. It is time for you to move on with your life. That is good." He hesitated a little more and then asked, "Have you thought about what will happen to Gooseberry Farm? Who will buy it? It will take a little time to make plans for it to be sold and even more time before you will be able to move into number 28. A lot still has to be done. Do you know what you would like to happen to the farm, Tegan?" He asked her gently and compassionately.

"Well, I have thought much about it, Carter. I have watched and prayed it through, over these past weeks. Do you have any ideas that I might not have thought about or anything that I might not be aware of?" she asked. "I have never had to do anything like this before," she said quietly as she bowed her head, "I'm glad of your help."

Evie got up to make another cup of tea. She too thought that this was a right move for Tegan, and the best of it would be that she would still be in the village so they could keep up their close friendship.

"I think another cuppa, would go down just fine, don't you?"

she said, as she looked at Tegan and gave her a smile.

She began to pour the boiling water into the teapot once more. As they drank their tea together, Carter and Evie told Tegan that they would do all they could to help her and see her settled into her new home.

"I have not told the girls yet, Carter, but I think I will tell them later on tonight when it is quiet and we are by ourselves. I have one more thing to say though. I hope that when I have expressed what I am going to say next, that we will be able to do this together; all three of us." After a small sigh, she spoke what was on her heart.

"I have been watching Tommy and our Peggy over these past few years and I think that they are getting serious in their relationship. They are not just wee children anymore. They are in their late teens and I feel that Malachi would have agreed with what I am about to say. Malachi thought a lot of your Tommy. He said he was a hard working lad and he could trust him with anything. In the last year Tommy helped Malachi so much that he reckoned Tommy would be able to run this farm on his own. I know that Malachi would have been happy to let Tommy follow on from him, working this farm.

I would like, with your permission, to offer Gooseberry Farm to Tommy first, before I think about putting it on the market. Do you agree with me on this?" Tegan implored them.

For a minute Carter and Evie just looked at each other full of surprise and excitement and then Carter answered her.

"Well Tegan, I agree with you about our Tommy's capabilities. I suppose I hadn't thought about him owning his own farm yet but it is going to happen one of these days, I suppose."

He thought some more. "I think this is a really good idea. I am pleased that it is so near to us. We could continue to work together on both farms. Evie and I are delighted about this," he smiled at Evie, "but we will pray about it together and see what kind of finance can be arranged for him as well.

It is an answer to your problem and I'm sure it can be sorted. Let's just wait another week or so, before we tell our Tommy. We would not want to raise his hopes too soon. Let's ask God to show us if these plans are His plans too; His plans for Tommy's life," Carter said.

Tegan spoke up again. "Our Peggy and Tommy will marry,

don't you think? They are so close. What a lovely home it would be for them. I would be so happy to see them settled there, and I know they will be so happy together. Just like Malachi and I were," her voice softened, a sort of 'keeping it in the family'!

As they sat quietly together they were amazed at how the afternoon had turned out. Yes, Tommy and Peggy, they were sure, were an item! It was looking as if they would be together as a couple. Oh, what fantastic news to be able to give them. And oh how lovely for Tegan and Patience to be moving into number 28, Church Road! They would still be close neighours.

They bowed their heads together to ask their heavenly Father to give them His blessing on all of this and to comfort and to strengthen Tegan, as this would be such a big change for her. They asked God to prepare Tommy's and Peggy's hearts too. They acknowledged their loving Heavenly Father in all of this and were assured that He would make a way for them to know His plans for each one of their lives.

Chapter 5. **Plans Unfolded!**

Over the following weeks Carter, Evie and Tegan did much planning and preparation for the move and for handing over of the farm to Tommy.

Tegan arranged plans for number 28, Church Road and the deal was made. The cottage had been empty for a long while. Work was needed to be done on the property and the garden needed tidying up. They would start it straight away.

Tommy and Peggy were unaware of what their parents were up to. They both continued to enjoy being together and Tommy was building up enough confidence to ask Peggy to marry him.

They were both nearing the age of twenty now although Peggy was a few months younger than Tommy. 'I love Peggy,' he thought. However there was always a reserve in his heart when he thought about marrying her. He could not help but think back to that day when she had said that they were 'just mates' and someone else would come along and 'sweep her off her feet one day'! And yet, they enjoyed each other's company so much, didn't they? What would he do without Peggy?

He didn't want to think about that now though. He would soon ask Peggy to marry him. Yes he must do so, before he lost her to someone else!

Peggy and Patience were chatting in their bedroom a few nights later. Patience asked her sister about how things were going between Tommy and her.

Peggy answered, "I think I have fallen in love with Tommy. We get on so well. We don't struggle with conversation, we enjoy the same things, and I can't wait for the evenings when Tommy and I can just have time to go for a walk, or spend time on our own. We always talk about what God is showing us, and enjoy being in church, hearing more from the Bible which teaches us and helps us to know the direction God wants for our lives. I think God is drawing us together, Patience. I feel so happy and Tommy is so happy with working out on the farm I know. Helping out his father sometimes and working on our farm here, it really suits him.

Dad really liked Tommy and trusted him to do the work well. He is always singing and he is always joyful. I know he loves God. That is so important isn't it that we both have faith in God."

Patience had been watching Peggy; watching as her face lit up when she spoke about Tommy; Tommy, who she had grown up with throughout their childhood years. Who would have thought it? But she had also noticed how they were sharing secrets together and quietly whispering in the corner of the room, or going out for walks by themselves, or laughing away in each other's company, especially when they thought no-one was watching them. They were so happy together. That was obvious to everyone.

"Well, I can see that you both get on so well, it's not really a surprise our Peg. I don't suppose anyone would be surprised about you two, when I think about it!" Patience said.

"As for me, I don't think Edward Moreton has even thought twice about me. We come out of church each week and he just smiles at me, says a quick hello and then he's off again! How will I ever get him to notice me enough to even want to go out with me? Do you think he likes me, just a little, our Peg?" Patience asked her sister.

"I don't know, but he is a nice lad, and he is a Christian as well. Let's ask God to show you and bless you in this. We know that the Bible tells us that it is right for believers to go out with another Christian, because God says it is important to marry someone who believes the same as we do and desires the same things as we do. We want to do the right thing and be in God's will."

Both girls then prayed together and asked God to confirm to them that Tommy was the one for Peggy, and for Edward to ask Patience out on a date.

Now they would just have to wait and see what would happen next Sunday at church.

"I do hope Edward will be there," Patience said. "I hope that I will get a chance to speak with him and see if he shows an interest in me. I really like him Peggy, I really do."

The next day, Tommy was waiting to see if Peggy would come out into the yard to call him in for tea. He gently worked away at what he was doing with the animals, and hoped deep inside him, that he would have an opportunity to talk with Peggy, alone. He had prayed about their relationship and he knew it was now or never! But still he had a little niggle deep inside him that she might turn him down. He would have to trust in his God - and have enough confidence to do what he so wanted to do, which was to ask Miss Peggy Norman to marry him, Tommy Fearne!

There was one problem though! Where would they live? How would Tegan feel about losing one of her daughters? How would she feel if they moved away from the village? The more he thought about it, the more he knew that he would have to live close to both sets of parents, for they needed his help. Also, Tegan would miss Peggy too much if they married and moved far away. He would have to pray about it some more!

Tommy remembered his favourite text, the one Rev. Malcolm had preached on a few years ago.

'Seek ye first the kingdom of God and all these things shall be added unto you.'

He knew that God had directed him to seek Him in all things. He did not want to live his life without asking God about His plans for his life. He knew that serving God first would give him peace and hope.

So knowing this, he bowed his head and prayed and sought his heavenly Father's direction. He would trust Him today. He was going to ask Peggy if she would marry him and he wasn't going to wait any longer!

His wish came true. Peggy came out of the kitchen door and called him in for tea.

"Tommy," she called, "Tommy, tea is ready. Where are you?" She ran across the yard and caught up with him. "Do you want your tea now, Tommy? Ma has set it on the table. Come away in."

Tommy was delighted. "Peg, do you think you will be able to come out later and go for a walk with me this evening. It would be nice to spend the evening together and then you can come home with me after, to Beech Farm for a cup of tea."

"Aw, Tommy," she reached up and gave him a quick kiss on his cheek, "I would love to. What time will you be ready for me?"

"I will just feed the cattle and shut in the hens and then we will go for a walk down the lane." He grabbed her hand and they ran into the kitchen together. They mustn't be late for tea!

That evening at 7 o'clock they were walking down the lane when they came to their favourite place by a stile at the side of the brook. The sound of the running water which was trickling by was beautiful and calming. They found a nice place to sit down and look at the scene around them. The trees were majestic and they both enjoyed the quietness of the countryside. There were some birds flying high in the sky above the trees, singing away to their Maker.

"I really miss my da, Tommy. Sometimes I just think about him and I feel so lost without him." She held onto Tommy's hand tightly. "How will I ever get over the loss of him in my life? Da meant such a lot to me. He was so kind. Ma is ever so brave as well. She just keeps on going. I know that it is her faith, and her very good friends that help keep her strong. But I do hear her quietly crying in her room sometimes. She misses Da, so much too," said Peggy sadly.

"I know lass. It is hard. I miss him as well. When I need advice I miss him. I remember Malachi before he got so ill, and I think about all the advice he gave to me then and I still try to do what I know he would have wanted me to do on the farm. I love the farm Peg, just as if it were mine," he answered her, softly.

"Tommy, we are so blessed to be living here, aren't we? Just think of all those people who do not know what fresh air is! And thank you Tommy so much, for being here for me and for holding me when I need you. I don't know what I would have done without you, you know."

"Peg, I am so glad that we have been friends for as long as I can remember. I will always try to be here for you," he said gently, "always."

"I know. You are wonderful," she answered him. She stood up and walked along the side of the stream a little, watching the water trickling gently over the pebbles.

"Can you remember when we were younger and we used to paddle in this stream and have picnics with all the others? I know shall we plan one again soon Tommy; all of our Sunday school group together? I know that Patience would like to invite Edward Moreton along. She quite likes him really, but nothing is happening yet in that direction. Would you like that Tommy - a group picnic together?" she enquired.

"I would like to do anything that makes you happy, Peg. Now hush. I would like to ask you something myself! Do you remember how we always seem to find solace in each other? With everything that has happened, we always end up together, sharing our grief and our joys. I enjoy your company and I was wondering if you felt the same about me, Peg. Do you enjoy being with me, just the two of us?"

"Of course I do, Tommy. Isn't that what I have just been

saying?" she answered him, "You are always here for me, and I love it."

"Peg, I want us to be married. I do love you. I want to be there for you, always. I want to be there to love you and to hold you, and to take care of you. I feel that your da would have been happy about this. I know that he would have been very happy to know that I would be taking care of you. I love you and I think I always have; even when we were little and messing around with the others. There was always something different about our friendship. Will you marry me, Peg, darling?" Tommy asked.

Tommy got down from sitting on the stile and walked over to her and knelt on one knee at her feet. "Will you marry me our Peggy?"

"Why, Tommy. Yes, Yes, Yes! I love you." She threw her arms around him and gave him a very big kiss. Then there was nothing else to say, for the hug and kiss had said it all!

Peggy was so happy. She couldn't contain it. She wanted no one else to take this happiness away from her.

Tommy couldn't believe that he had just proposed! Wow! God had given him the strength he needed to ask her. Thank you God, he prayed silently. And he couldn't believe that she had accepted his proposal either. Is this really happening to me he wondered?

"Peg, thank you. I was hoping that you would agree to marry me. Shall we just thank God and ask His blessing on our lives together."

There, by the side of that brook, they knelt down holding hands, asking God to overshadow them and to bless them and be in their plans for their future.They thanked God for bringing them together and for giving them this special love, this love that would last until their dying day. Of that they were sure!

Happily and holding hands, they ran up the lane into the farmhouse and burst in through the kitchen door making such an awful din!

Chapter 6. **The News!**

A week ago Carter, Evie and Tegan thought that as things had progressed and they could now see a few loose ends tying up, they would speak to Tommy on his own and lay out their plans before him. Then they would tell the girls, after Tommy had made up his mind about taking on Gooseberry Farm. But Tommy would need to know what was on their minds first.

Sitting cosily in the kitchen on the easy chairs either side of the Rayburn, Tegan and Evie were enjoying an evening of darning socks and chatting about the wonderful things God was doing in their church. They were overjoyed that many families were coming in and they sat planning an evening to get them all together for fellowship in Evie's home.

Darning socks seemed to be one of their usual tasks after supper! In fact, any excuse for meeting up and having a chat was good. The men were heavy on their socks, with holes appearing all the time. It seemed a never ending job. So Tegan kindly helped Evie with this task as often as she could. Evie loved spending her evenings with her two very best friends in her home.

Carter was sat at the table doing some paperwork and sorting out the bills. Evie was always happy to be near her husband. They were sitting there in the quiet when Tommy and Peggy hurtled into the kitchen holding hands, looking radiant and as if they were about to burst!

"Ma, when did you come over here?" Peggy asked Tegan, full of surprise. "When we left after tea, you were going to do some ironing!"

"I decided that it was better to come over and see Evie, than sit there all by myself. Both you and Patience were out, so here I am. What is all the fuss and noise about then?" she asked them both looking first at Tommy and then back to Peggy.

Tommy and Peggy exchanged looks and both shouted out at the same time, "We are engaged."

Their parents tried to look surprised. Tegan looked at Evie laughing and Evie looked at Carter and all of them burst into joyous laughter.

"See, I told you," Tegan exclaimed, "I knew they were keen on each other."

God bless you both," she said as Peggy came over, and gave her mother a big hug. She then went over to Evie, to hug her and then back to Carter. Carter stood up and shook his son's hand and then congratulated them both.

Carter spoke up for all of them and told Tommy and Peggy they were delighted with their news and that they would all be looking forward to a wedding in the near future where they would celebrate their love!

"As you know Ma, we left home to go for a walk when Tommy surprised me," Peggy said excitedly. "Down by the stile over the brook, he asked me to marry him. I am so happy Ma. I am so happy that everyone here, all of you," she looked at her Ma and then at Tommy's parents in turn, "are pleased with our news. Thank you all so much. I can't wait to see our Patience and tell her the news as well. I am so happy, Ma!" She did a little skip up and down and Tommy burst out laughing. She could not contain her excitement!

There were lots of looks and winks between their parents then, which neither Tommy nor Peggy noticed for they were caught up in their own happiness. Carter and Evie were looking at Tegan for her to present their news to this happy couple. It seemed like now was the right time to tell them what was going on and there was no time like the present! As they had hoped this news had come just at the right time to enable Tegan to share more freely her own news with them.

"Well, it seems this is the night for news then," Tegan said, "We are delighted with your news, Peggy and Tommy, but we have some news of our own to tell you." As Tegan spoke to them she looked across at her friends and felt their total support.

Tommy and Peggy came and sat down with their parents and listened quietly until Tegan had finished her story. She told them about her moving to 28, Church Road in the village and the reason why she felt it was the right time to move.

Carter then continued to tell them the rest of the story.

"And there is more to come," he began, "Gooseberry Farm will need someone to buy it and to run it. We have been talking it over and have decided that we would offer it to you Tommy and now to Peggy too; for you both to think over the possibility of owning Gooseberry Farm yourselves and making it your own place. There are still lots of details to go through, and of course there are more plans to make, but what do you think?"

Tommy and Peggy were astounded! They couldn't quite take it all in. All this news they had received in just a few short hours and all of it so momentous. But there was no need to think about it anymore. They both felt it in their hearts that this was God's blessing on their marriage. They were delighted.

"Da, is it possible? Gooseberry Farm - ours? We have only just got engaged," they burst out laughing. "Is this really happening to us?"

After a short while, everyone calmed down and Carter looked at his son again and spoke to him quietly,

"Tommy, we know you are a sensible boy. Malachi would have been overjoyed to have known that his lovely daughter and her husband were the ones to take over his farm, and he would know it would be safe in your hands. Your mother and I are so proud of you, proud of you both," he said as he looked at Peggy.

"Tegan has expressed her desire that you should do what you want with it as long as you care for it and make it your own. It will be your's and Peggy's home now Tommy if that is what you would like?"

"Thank you Da. This is such a blessing; one I am not worthy of, but I, or should I say 'we', are so thankful and grateful for you all for helping us like this. Yes, we would love to move into Gooseberry Farm. Thank you."

It took the rest of the evening together for all of this news to sink in with Tommy and Peggy; indeed with the whole family. Tonight had brought its own news and together it all seemed to fit like a glove. God did indeed answer prayer and go before them.

When it was time for Tegan and Peggy to return to their home, Carter reached up to the shelf for his Bible and began to read from Matthew chapter 6, verses 19 - 34. Their Family Altar time was here again. The reading consisted of the Lord Jesus saying to the people who were surrounding Him, not to store up treasures on earth but to store up treasures in heaven, *'For where your treasure is, there will your heart be always'*, Jesus said.

The chapter went on to speak about not worrying about things, *'For God knows what you need and just as He cares for the sparrows, He will take care of you'*.

And then Tommy was amazed again when his da, read out

his own special verse at the end of the chapter. *'But seek ye first the kingdom of God and all these things shall be added unto you,'*

"Wow, God. Thank you." Tommy now knew God's seal upon all the news that had been shared that night. God was adding to his life much more than he could ever have thought!

Carter then closed his Bible and prayed a prayer of thanks to the God who cares for everybody, even them.

As Tommy said goodbye to Peggy that night he shared with her his own special verse. They knew that as they had asked God about their relationship and as they had listened to Him and obeyed Him, He was now adding blessings on their future together.

My, what news they had received that night. From being on their own, they were now going to be a couple. They had got a place to live, with their parents living nearby.

Yes, thought Tommy, this is the verse that will take me through my life, and as I choose to seek God first with all of my heart, I know Peggy and I will continue to seek Him together in all that we do.

"Goodnight lass. I will see you tomorrow. Sleep well and sweet dreams my lovely," he said as he waved Peggy and Tegan goodbye later that evening.

Tegan and Peggy soon were arriving back home to tell Patience all the wonderful things that had happened over the last few hours. Was all this really happening? They were both ecstatic! What a wonderful day of good news for them all!

Chapter 7. **The Picnic**

After the service had ended the following Sunday, everyone gathered around Tommy and Peggy to congratulate them on the news of their engagement. All their friends were excited but no-one was surprised at all. Tommy and Peggy had always seemed as if they were meant to be together! Lots of noise and laughter and well wishes were going on.

Patience noticed Edward Moreton over the other side of the room so she went over to talk with him. At first she was a little shy but as she approached him, he saw her coming and turned to speak with her first.

“What lovely news of your Peggy and Tommy, Patience. When do you think the wedding will be? I always knew that one day those two would get married.”

“I know,” answered Patience. ”It’s all so exciting isn’t it? The wedding will be soon I know that. They can’t wait to be married. I am so happy for them both.”

“Would you like to join me for a cup of tea, Patience? I’m just going to have one over there,” Edward asked her nervously as he was making his way across to the counter.

“Thank you that would be very nice.” she replied.

How her heart missed a beat inside her. Was this really happening to her? Was she really going for a drink with Edward? She felt herself all aglow!

During their conversation she found herself telling Edward all about the group picnic that she and Peggy were trying to organise in a few weeks. She talked about their favourite spot down by the stile and by the brook and wondered if he thought that would be a good place to hold the group picnic.

Edward said that he would be pleased to join them and would look forward to it. Patience felt hope stir within her again. Maybe there was a chance for her and Edward after all! ‘Thank you Lord,’ she said quietly.

Later on that evening when she was back at home with Peggy she told her about her time with Edward that day and the invitation that she had given him to the picnic.

Peggy and Patience were even more excited and continued to make further plans for this ‘get together’. This was going to be a special day they knew.

God had heard their prayers in their bedroom a little while ago when they had prayed together about Tommy and Edward and their relationships. God was going before them and they were so blessed.

Lots of arrangements were needed to be made for the picnic. 'Who shall we invite? We mustn't miss anyone out! When shall we plan this for? It must be when most people can make it.'

"Shall we do the planning and just let others come and enjoy the day?" Patience said. "I love organising and it would be nice for the others to come and enjoy!"

"I think it would be nice to have the whole group from church and invite some of our new friends along too," Peggy said.

They soon made a list of all the people to invite and arranged the picnic for two weeks on Saturday.

"Let's go and find our Tommy and see what he has to say about this," Peggy said, as they walked through to the kitchen where Tommy was sitting on his own, deep in thought!

Patience couldn't wait for this day to arrive. She was going to see Edward again and she was hopeful, praying that this was the beginning of what she hoped would be a special friendship with Edward. He really was so handsome you know!

Edward Moreton was one of their original group of young people at the church. They had always known each other and she had kept it a secret that she liked him. Yes, this had been her secret. Only Peggy knew what she felt about Edward.

Edward had never moved away from the village. When he left school he became one of the teachers in the school in which he had been as a pupil himself, in Maxwell. He was a popular member of the staff and also among the pupils. He cared for each child and gave them as much attention as he could.

Edward was a little older than Patience by two years and was now well established in the school. He loved his job and felt secure in his work. School life was his passion.

Edward's other passion was serving his Lord in the church in Maxwell. He was a deacon in this church and filled this position with great enthusiasm.

Every time there was a service or event on, he would go ahead and sort out all the preparations for arranging the church and making sure everything was put into place. He was a faithful deacon.

Tommy was pleased with all the plans and arrangements the girls had made for this special group picnic. He helped them to arrange some practical items for this and promised that the others would come along and help as well.

The day soon arrived and early on that Saturday morning Tommy and some of the lads took tables and chairs down to the picnic site. This day was a bright sunny day with a slight breeze. It was perfect and they all felt that this was God's blessing on their gathering together.

Twelve o'clock came and with all the food prepared and set up to look as appetising as possible, everyone started to arrive with a feeling of anticipation.

How good it was to celebrate this Saturday afternoon together. It would be a time of sharing, laughter, encouragement and friendship.

Archie, Edward, Tommy and the boys decided that a game of rounders would be good, so they organised different teams of players including many of the girls. They had so much fun together.

After having some cold drinks to cool them down, Mary and Peggy decided to go for a short walk alongside the trickling brook. Mary and Peggy were closest friends. They enjoyed chatting away in the beauty of their surroundings. They were so happy. This was indeed a special day. Soon they found that the others girls were joining them and the conversation changed to Peggy's forthcoming wedding!

Lots of talk of wedding dresses, bridesmaid's dresses and all the colours they were choosing, and many other plans were discussed. It was all so intriguing and interesting. Peggy had such a lovely group of trusted friends surrounding her that nothing could spoil anything. Her day was getting even more wonderful! But this day, the day of the picnic came to an end all too soon!

The whole group gathered back together by the stile and decided to finish their day off with a time of praise and thanks to God for His faithfulness to each of them.

They enjoyed singing songs from their Sunday school days and of course they would have to sing their favourite song again, wouldn't they. How could they not sing this song?

They joined all their voices together and sang out with gusto, '*All things bright and beautiful'*, once more, having their own individual memories of days gone by.

They sang some more of their favorite songs together and then joined hands in prayer asking God to bless them and to continue to guide each of them, for all of their lives.

Later on that evening Peggy asked Patience how things were going between her and Edward.

"Oh, Peg I have had such a wonderful day. The picnic has been such a great success for us all. Edward enjoyed the game of rounders with the boys and we also had some time to talk with each other on our own. Do you know what? Edward has asked me to join him in school next week for sports day. He asked me if I would like to go in and help him set up the games. Would I like to go and help? What a silly question! I *can't wait* to go in and see him again!"

"I'm so pleased for you Patience. It looks like you two are getting on just fine. God is good. Maybe Edward is not so shy after all," Peggy exclaimed!

"I know, isn't it wonderful and this all started with a short prayer and an invite to join him for a cup of tea after church," Patience said amazed.

Both of their thoughts went straight to God to thank Him for blessing them so much. Yes, they thought, everything works together for good when you bring it to the Lord in prayer. Praying about everything is allowing God to come in and bring His plans to pass in our lives. And they so wanted his plans for them, for His plans are the very best!

They would now wait and see these plans being worked out. God would show them – He would not let them down.

Chapter 8. **New Beginnings!**

The day soon came for Tegan and Patience to move out of Gooseberry Farm and into their new home in the village. Tegan was a wee bit apprehensive but was also assured that this was right for her and for Patience too, so they busily started to move their belongings and have them taken down to their new home.

Number 28, Church Road, was already being prepared for their coming, with Evie and Carter and many others from their church busily helping them by taking care of the delivering and setting in place of the larger pieces of furniture.

However, with the task soon completed, Evie and Tegan sat down for a well-earned rest. They would leave the unpacking of the many other smaller boxes for tomorrow they thought.

As they were enjoying their cup of tea together they both sat quietly and prayed. They thanked God for all of His blessings to them.

"You know, Evie, I think I shall give number 28, a name. I think it deserves to have a name, don't you?" Tegan asked. "I feel it's like home already for me. I feel so blessed to have you, my very dear friends nearby and of course Tommy and Peggy will be in the old farmhouse a little way along the road. I feel that my heart is so full of joy. Yes, I am still a little sad that my dear Malachi is not here with me in this cottage, but I know I shall be happy here, because God surrounds me and I know that I am safe in His care. I still have many precious memories of my dear Malachi. I will still be living in the same village, surrounded by God and by my family and all of my friends.

I was thinking, Evie - do you like the name 'Keita'? I heard it only the other day actually. I felt it settle in my heart right then and now that I am here, it feels so right to call this cottage 'Keita'. Evie what do you think? Do you like the name 'Keita'?"

Evie listened to her friend and could see that it was important that she would be happy and settled in her new home. She knew that this would be a way of giving her some peace and security, and would of course make the cottage her very own.

"Yes, Tegan, I do like that name," she hesitated a little, giving her more time to think. "Yes; 'Keita'. That sounds just right. Do you know the meaning of Keita, Tegan? Although I like it, I have not heard the name before."

"Well, I have looked it up and it originates from Scotland so I understand. It actually means an 'Enclosed Place.' I want my home to be a place that is closed in with God, Evie; a place where Patience and I will feel 'enclosed in' and secure in God's protection and care. It will be where we will know His presence, and a place where friends and family can come and visit our home and feel welcomed and loved. I want it to be a warm and welcoming home for everyone who calls to see us.

In Zechariah chapter 2:10 it says, *'Sing and rejoice, O daughter of Zion; for lo, I come and I dwell in the midst of you', says the Lord.'* You know, when Malachi and I came to visit you and Carter, we always knew we had been in God's presence after having spent time with you in your home. We would say to each other on the many occasions that we stepped into your kitchen, that it gave us such peace in our hearts that we actually felt it! I pray that people will experience that here in Keita. Thank you for showing us how to dwell with God and let God dwell with us, so it can reach out to others as well. You are such a blessing to me Evie. I thank God for you."

Evie hugged her friend and knew that God would indeed use this home to touch many people's lives in the future. "Yes," she said, "God will dwell here and people will call to see you and be blessed. Keita is absolutely the right name for number 28, I'm sure."

So a new home, with a new name, and a new start began that day for Tegan and Patience. A time for new beginnings, Tegan thought, as she waved goodbye to her dearest friend a little later on that night, when Evie left to walk the short distance back to her home at Beech Farm.

And maybe it was a time of new beginnings for Patience and Edward too!

Tommy and Peggy were married during the summer of 1952. Their wedding was just beautiful with a lovely family time of celebration together as they celebrated their special love in the reception with their close friends and family. Lots of speeches were made and everyone was so happy.

Peggy had looked stunning in her white satin wedding dress and the long trailing veil. She wore the pearls around her neck that Tommy had saved up to buy for her. These pearls were special and they looked so beautiful on her, along with her pearl-drop earrings which had been a gift to her from her mother at the time of their engagement. Tommy had given her the pearls as a significant promise to her on the day of their wedding, that from today she would be promised to him for always.

The name Peggy means 'pearl and promise' and he had indeed found his own pearl and had promised her his love forever and for always!

Patience and Mary were their bridesmaids. They walked down the aisle side by side and stood at the front looking like brides themselves in their pale blue dresses, carrying small bouquets of carnations and white lilies.

Carter had the privilege of walking Peggy down the aisle to meet her bridegroom. He felt honoured when Peggy had asked him to give her away. He felt proud to be standing in Malachi's place. Peggy had been like a daughter to him for a long time now. How this day would have meant so much to Malachi he thought, but Malachi would not be forgotten. He gave her his biggest, widest smile and with Peggy on his arm they both made a beautiful entrance into the church when the bells rang out.

Tommy's face was radiant as he turned and looked at his bride who was entering the church with Carter at her side, walking slowly up the aisle towards him. How stunning she looked! He would soon repeat the vows that would make her his wife. He loved her so much!

In his speech at the reception, which was just a small buffet, he told everyone there, that God had given him the most beautiful girl in the world to be his wife. He gave a small tribute to Malachi and Peggy thought that she could not love him any more than at that moment, for her heart was overflowing with joy.

Life for Mr. and Mrs. Tommy Fearne was just beginning, and my how they looked forward to all that was before them. They were so happy, so very happy!

Now it was time for them both to settle down on their very own farm. It all seemed like a dream to them but they knew that God was blessing them abundantly and they gave Him thanks for everything that day.

They were going to make sure that the Family Altar time in the evenings would continue in their own home. How could they let a day go by without thanking God for His care for them? It was now Tommy's responsibility to keep this time special in their lives. They both loved their God and would serve Him every day that they lived.

Everything had been arranged for them to move into the farmhouse as soon as they were back from their honeymoon break. Now that they were Mr. and Mrs. Tommy Fearne of Gooseberry Farm, Tommy could hardly take it all in.

Again his favourite verse of scripture came into his mind. *'Seek ye first the Kingdom of God and all these things shall be added unto you.'*

"Thank you, Lord," he prayed, "for adding to me and giving to me such a wonderful wife, and for our new home and for our new life here on this farm. We will serve you and put you first, always.

'Take my life and let it be, consecrated Lord to Thee. Take my moments and my days; let them flow in ceaseless praise.' He sang out the words quietly and prayerfully to His faithful God.

"Take our lives Lord. We will live for you together in Gooseberry Farm. May our home be, as my parents' home has always been in the past, a safe haven for us and for those that you will send to us in the future. Thank you God," he prayed.

Tommy and Peggy lived for each other every day and they grew in their faith together and as they did so, their love for each other deepened.

They had many friends come and visit them in their home and as time went on, God did indeed bring in many people who needed to hear that God loved them also.

Gooseberry Farm was a loving environment as Tommy and Peggy were delighted to serve their God right there, where He had placed them, as husband and wife.

Gooseberry Farm came alive again with new life and a new purpose. New beginnings for Gooseberry Farm and for its new owners!

Chapter 9. **Home**

Peggy was quite good at arranging flowers and making things look pretty. She had the gift of making their new house into a home. Everywhere was cosy, comfortable and welcoming. On the wall in the kitchen was a picture with Tommy's special Bible verse on it. It pictured a young couple going up the path into a church, arm in arm, about to worship God. They were going to seek God's guidance for the week that was before them. That picture said so much more to them both the more they looked at it. '*Seek ye first the Kingdom of God'* was inscribed along the bottom of the picture. It would always be their own special calling, to put God first and to never forget Him.

In the future as they lived their daily lives, they would turn their eyes to this picture many times and through all that they would experience, God would speak its truth deep into their hearts, time and time again.

Peggy was pleased with the finished result of all her endeavours. Now everything was in its place it felt like home - hers and Tommy's. But she would ever be mindful that once this kitchen had been her childhood home, with her mother, father and sister. Then it was Mother's kitchen, but now it was her own, her very own to both work in and to enjoy every day with Tommy.

Upstairs they had chosen the bedroom at the front of the farmhouse to be their own. They could see the path up to the front of the house from this window enabling them to see when visitors came to their door. Their room was painted a pale green colour and in the opposite two bedrooms the wallpaper was light and bright.

The bedroom that she and Patience had shared was at the back of the house. This room held so many memories for her. Good memories of course and whenever Patience would need to stay with them, she could sleep in this room and share the same memories.

Tommy was getting used to the fact that this was now his farm and he was no longer just going in to work for Malachi. He thought that Malachi had worked the farm well but he was now ready to make a few changes and make it his very own!

He had been so pleased to realise that he was now in charge of the farm and all the responsibility was now on his shoulders. He loved nothing else than being out in the fresh air and working with the animals.

Tommy himself was a keen gardener as well as loving his farm work, so he was planning on making a very large area to grow vegetables and plant some fruit bushes. This would help to increase his income.

He tidied up the outhouses and the buildings and arranged to have a new greenhouse placed at the bottom of the garden where he would put in a little gate for easier access out of the yard.

Tommy regularly checked over his farm equipment and tools to see that they were kept clean and serviced.

He loved his tractor and trailer and the other equipment he had, to help plough fields and plant grain and he was increasingly satisfied with all that he was accomplishing at Gooseberry Farm.

Carter was a great help and encouragement to him advising him when it was best to plant, sow and then reap and harvest the crops.

Carter had shown Tommy throughout his young years how to run and manage a farm and how to maintain the equipment to keep things running smoothly and efficiently. Tommy would not go wrong if he followed in his father's footsteps!

Carter was a very good farmer who was much respected by everyone in the local community. Carter kept very good health and remained strong even though he was now getting older.

Evie was healthy too. She enjoyed her work for the church and her times with Tegan at Keita. Even though time was running away in front of their eyes they still had much to accomplish for the Lord and for their children.

Not long after they had settled into the farm, Evie decided to call and see how her son and daughter-in-law were getting on. It was a beautiful day so she walked from Beech Farm along the road and up the path to knock on their kitchen door. Peggy saw her coming towards the house and she opened the door to invite her mother-in-law inside.

"Mrs. Fearne, please come in. I will make some tea for you. Tommy will be in soon and we can have a cuppa together," she said. "Thank you so much for coming to see us."

Evie walked in and sat in the armchair as directed. "Why lass, you have made this so cosy and homely already," she exclaimed as she looked around her taking in the neatness and the orderliness of the room. "We are so pleased for you both," Evie said, "and it's lovely to see you so happy."

After pouring hot water into the teapot Peggy reached up for two cups and saucers and poured the milk into the cups.

"I do think that you can call me 'Evie' or even 'Ma' now Peggy," Evie said to her daughter-in-law. "It's so nice for us to all be part of the same family at last."

"Thank you Evie. Yes. I love being part of your family. I always thought it would be nice to belong to your family and that Tommy was so lucky to have you and Carter as his parents and to live in Beech Farm. Beech Farm has been like my second home.

I hope that you know that you are welcome here as well and feel that you can come at any time to visit us," she said invitingly.

Peggy passed Evie her cup of tea and as she looked out of the window she noticed that Tommy was walking up the path towards the house, "I will just pour Tommy his drink. He's on his way inside, Evie. He must have seen you coming up the drive."

"Tommy, look who has come to visit us," she said, as she nodded her head towards Evie. Tommy had already stepped into the kitchen and had begun to take off his working boots. As he did so, he smiled across at his wife and then walked across to the armchair to where his Mother was sitting already looking comfortable. He bent down to give her a kiss on the cheek.

"Ma, it's so lovely to see you today. How are things at home? Is Da still working out in the meadow?" he turned his head. "Thank you lass," he said to Peggy as she handed him his cup of tea.

They sat chatting and drinking their tea together and then Evie handed Peggy a parcel. "For you Peggy as I promised you," she said lovingly.

Peggy opened the parcel slowly. As she tore away the wrapping she saw the willow patterned plate inside the package and she jumped for joy. She turned it over where she saw her name written on the back. She remembered that Evie had written it there a few years ago when she had put it aside for such a time as this.

"Thank you, Evie, thank you so much. Look our Tommy, just like your Ma promised me that day back at Beech Farm," she said. "Evie said I could have it as my very own when I got married. I don't think either of us knew then, just *who* I was going to marry," she laughed out loud. "But I'm so glad it's you I married, our

Tommy, to keep this in the family so to speak!" she said, as she held it up proudly for them all to see.

Peggy gave her mother-in-law a kiss and went to put the plate onto the table. She would think later where she was going to finally put it. How kind Evie was she thought quickly to herself, but then Peggy had always known that. She had always liked her mother-in-law even as a little girl!

Evie stayed a little longer with them and after a while she decided to leave and call in to visit Tegan on her way home, as she was passing her cottage. "Bye then you two. See you on Sunday," she called out to them, as she headed off down the path, her heart happy and full. "God bless you both."

As Evie continued to walk down the road she counted her many blessings. She thanked God for all of her family and for her best friend, Tegan. How good it was to be able to live near each other and be able to help each other whenever they needed it. Evie had enjoyed helping Tegan and Patience move into Church Road a few months earlier.

Again she considered the name of the house again. She was pleased to stop at Keita, and make a visit to see her very dear friend. She knew she would be welcome!

Church on Sundays continued to be the same for them all. Such occasions were family times together where each of them could look forward to meeting up to worship this God who had provided for them in so many wonderful ways. They had much evidence of that, right before their very eyes.

Rev. Malcolm gave another good sermon that day which had given them much food for thought. The pastor would pay regular visits to each of their homes and he would remind his flock of 'Jesus, The Good Shepherd' who always cared for His flock.

Rev. Malcolm loved to serve the Lord by caring for his flock too. He appreciated that ensuring the safe keeping of the people in his congregation who felt loved and cared for, would also ensure they would be open to receive more from God and grow in their faith as they felt the love of 'The True Shepherd' touching them.

Chapter 10. **Family Life.**

Tommy and Peggy continued to enjoy life on the farm. A few more years passed and Tommy had succeeded in getting his own garden plan underway where all the produce was grown and taken to the market every week to be sold. All was going well. The animals were strong and healthy and were being productive. They sold well in the markets and farming was very pleasing to Tommy.

Carter thoroughly enjoyed watching and helping his son make the farm fruitful but there was one thing that was beginning to worry him. Tommy continued to work hard but there were times when he would wince in pain but would try not to show that he was suffering. Carter also noticed that Tommy was finding it difficult to dig in the garden and to lift heavy weights. At first he tried not to notice it thinking that he was imagining it, but as time went on Tommy would wince more often as he worked. He wondered what was going on but decided to approach Tommy about it when the time was right. He didn't want to interfere in his life but he did keep Tommy in his prayers. He prayed much for their home, for their lives and for the wonderful news that they had recently received, that he was going to be a grandad in the near future! He took his concerns and his cares to the Lord trusting that God would take care of them.

Carter often went home at night to sit in his favourite chair in the kitchen by the warmth of the Rayburn. Lately he would sit quietly with a concerned look on his face. Evie noticed that there was something worrying him but she refrained from asking him for a while. However, as this continued each night, she turned to her husband one evening and asked him.

"Carter, what is worrying you? I have noticed that there is something on your mind when you come in every evening and sit in your chair. Are you all right, my love?"

"Well, lass, I have been watching our Tommy and I feel that there is something wrong with him. He seems to be suffering in some way. Over the past few months he has been struggling with the work. He tries not to let me see it but I do notice, Evie. It is on my mind a lot particularly these last few days."

Evie was shocked. "Why didn't you tell me, Carter? You should not keep things like this from me. We need to ask God to help him and we need to ask Tommy what the problem is and see how we can help him ourselves. I have noticed myself recently, that when he sits down he gives a little groan. I have just put it down to him being overtired and exhausted, but maybe it is a bigger problem than we both realise," she said sadly.

"He is doing so well Evie and he loves that farm of his. He is always grateful to God for everything he has. He thanks God for all the profit he makes and for the evident blessing on the crops that are grown there. He never takes anything for granted. I am so proud of him, Evie, so proud of them both," Carter said quietly, "but I do hope that there is nothing seriously wrong with him."

They both read from the Bible that night and with heavy hearts they brought their son and daughter-in-law to their heavenly Father. They thanked God for the news of their future grandchild and trusted God to bless them all and to meet their needs, especially Tommy's!

Soon, some wonderful news came to them early one morning. They woke to the sound of Tommy knocking on their front door with the news of their little new grandchild having been born during the night. Baby Rachel Pearl Fearne was born and all was well. Peggy and Rachel were now safely tucked up in bed and sleeping. Carter and Evie could come later on that day and visit their new grand-daughter and check that all was well with Peggy.

After he had left Beech Farm Tommy knocked on the door of Keita and then gently opened it and called out to Tegan, "Hello Tegan, are you there?"

Tegan walked out of the hallway and met Tommy in the kitchen. She knew straightaway what he was going to tell her. His face was beaming - he couldn't be more proud. He didn't really have to say anything to her but she let him tell her the news anyway!

"It's a girl! Mother and baby are doing well. Rachel Pearl was born in the early hours of this morning and they are both resting and sleeping now. You are now a grandmother, Tegan. Congratulations!" he said, as he embraced his mother-in-law.

Tegan called up to Patience who was already running down the stairs, when she heard all the commotion going on – she was now an aunty. How wonderful! They were all so excited. Later that day they would pop up to the farmhouse to see the wonderful new addition to the Fearne family.

Tommy then left and went home to his own little family. As

usual he thanked his God for the wonderful gift of a beautiful baby daughter.

Prior to the baby's birth Tommy and Peggy had decided that if their child was to be a little girl they would call her Rachel. Names were important to them both, so they knew their baby girl, their own wee precious lamb, would be aptly named 'Rachel', meaning 'lamb', with its spiritual meaning of innocence.

Every newborn baby is so sweet and pure and new and now their Rachel fitted the bill perfectly.

Now they were a complete family. Tommy had a wife and a daughter. He couldn't quite take it all in!

Peggy was delighted with their new arrival and proudly showed her off to the rest of the family when they all gathered together later on that day in their home. Carter took his place as head of the extended family and gave thanks for the safe delivery of his grand-daughter and prayed to God their heavenly Father, to bless and take care of them all.

Rachel Pearl Fearne was born on 8th July 1957, five years after their marriage. They were so happy and delighted with the safe arrival of their daughter that Tommy and Peggy felt that the joy of becoming a parent was the best feeling in the world! They marvelled at the miracle of new birth!

As time went on, Tommy and Peggy proved to be wonderful caring parents. They had both been brought up in Christian homes, so they had the wealth and knowledge of what it meant to love and cherish each other by letting their loved ones know how much they were loved by their parents as well as how much they were loved by God.

Rachel grew up to be such a happy and confident wee girl, safe in her parents love for her.

When she was a few weeks old, Rev. Malcolm dedicated her to the Lord in a special morning service in the local church. The church was packed out and Tommy and Peggy were so joyful. God had indeed added to their lives yet again!

In the next few months Peggy and Tommy were taking in all the changes in their little girl, watching her as she began to respond to their love and care for her and they were rewarded one day when her very own first smile and chuckle seemed to happen all at once!

Another day she surprised them both by saying 'Da' out

loud, when she raised her arms up to her father, to be lifted up. Tommy had never known such joy. His heart was overflowing!

Being parents to such a beautiful little girl was all they had ever wanted. They were going to do their very best in raising their daughter to grow up to love God the way they both loved Him, so that little Rachel would know God's special love too.

Chapter 11. **The Faithfulness of God**

However, from time to time Peggy noticed that Tommy winced as he picked up Rachel to cuddle her, even though he tried to hide it from everyone. She just prayed for him or tried to make it a little easier for him to hold her. She would encourage him to sit down first and then she would pass his daughter into his arms.

At the same time, Carter knew that it was time to talk with Tommy about things. He and Evie had asked God to undertake in the conversation when the time came to speak with their son.

Carter walked into the yard on a cold winter's day and saw Tommy walk toward the barn and step inside. He followed him in. He also noticed that Tommy looked so cold and tired and drawn.

"Hello Tommy. I just saw you come in here, lad. How are you today? Are all the animals fed and watered?" he called out to his son.

Tommy turned his head towards his father's voice. It was so good to hear him just then, he thought. It felt like being home. His father's company was what he needed right now!

"Hello Da. I didn't know you were behind me. It's bitterly cold today isn't it?" he said as he rubbed his hands together. He bent down and picked up a bale of straw.

"I'm just going to take this straw for bedding down the cows, and then I will be off back into the house into the warmth again to see my Peggy and wee Rachel."

As he did so, he tried to conceal the fact that it was difficult for him to lift up the bale of straw, but Carter noticed at once and took the opportunity to say something to him.

"Tommy, just a minute son. There is something that I want to ask you before we go back into the house. Do you mind lad, just staying out here for a second longer and then we can bed down the cows after? I want to ask you something. I've noticed over these past few months that you are in some kind of pain. Will you share with me what's troubling you lad? I don't want to interfere in your life but I want to help you in any way that I can," Carter said, "I can see there is something worrying you and things are not quite as they should be."

Tommy sat down on the bale of straw and was quite relieved in his heart. It would be good to speak with his father, he thought.

His da would help him with this.

He sighed! "Da, I am all right really, but I am having pain in my hip and in my back. I'm not sure what it is, but it is getting worse. I need to rest frequently and I am struggling with lifting things at times - but I am trying to cope. I hadn't realised that you knew anything though. I have thought it would get better by itself but it hasn't. I have also been praying for God to undertake in this problem for me. I know He is our present help in time of trouble so that is why I haven't bothered you with this, Da. But I think I do need to see the doctor now. What do you think Da?" Tommy looked up at his father seeking some reassurance that what he was doing was the right thing.

Carter was a little taken aback. So it was worse than he thought.

"Well lad, I think that now is the time to get it sorted. It's best not to let it go on any further without getting it checked out and don't struggle on without telling me when things are troubling you. I can help you even more on the farm now, if you let me Tommy. Does Peggy know about this?" Carter asked him gently.

Tommy told Carter that he had kept it all to himself as he didn't want to worry anyone and he had thought he was just a little stiff at times because he had been working so hard on the farm. He had reckoned it was due to overwork, especially at the beginning.

"Sometimes I catch her looking at me, Da and I think that she does notice something's not right, but then she gets caught up with our Rachel and she doesn't say anything to me about it."

"Well, now we must go in and tell her and make that doctor's appointment for you for tomorrow. I will do the feeding in the morning so you take yourself off along to the surgery, lad," Carter told his son, "You've no need to worry about things here."

When Tommy explained to Peggy about what was troubling him, she began to get upset, so he put his arms around her and told her that everything would be all right. They must trust God together. Peggy sat Rachel gently on his knee and they sought God together. They needed to pray first; that God would go before him and when he was to see the doctor, God would be in control of everything.

The next day Tommy went in to the surgery. He explained all of the problems he was having to his doctor. When he came out of the room a few minutes later he felt a little better in himself. The doctor had told him that it appeared to be that his hip was strained and overworked. He would need an x-ray to check how things were. Possibly he would need a new hip and then he would be free of pain. Tommy had hope in his heart again, but he had never given up on trusting God to bring him healing in all of this.

After the x-ray and some more tests on Tommy's back, hip and joints, surgery was planned for as soon as there was a free space available. It would take a couple of months before the operation but he did need a new hip.

The doctor told Tommy that he was suffering from arthritis even though he was only in his late twenties. It was really quite soon to need a hip operation but the heavy farm work which he had been doing since he was fourteen hadn't helped the situation. He had arthritis in his joints and particularly in his hips.

So Tommy didn't overdo it for the next few weeks and when the time came for his hip to be replaced, he went into hospital, leaving his precious family alone at home on the farm. He knew that his parents and Tegan would be there to help them, so he prayed with Peggy and Rachel for God to surround them and to love them and to keep them all safe in His care.

The operation was a success and Tommy was soon home again and surrounded by his family. He took care to rest and let his hip heal properly. He was glad to be free of much of the pain and soon he started to walk again. As he walked he was more upright than he had been for a while. The more he exercised, the better and stronger he got.

"It's so lovely to have you home again, Tommy. I never want to live without you. I missed you so much when you were in hospital, but I am pleased that you are better and can now be free of pain again. I asked God, just like we always do every day, to bless you and to heal you. I put God first in my prayers and I knew that He would take care of you and Rachel and me. He has never let us down yet, has He?" she declared confidently. "God is a faithful God and Father to us all of the time."

Tommy was delighted. He and Peggy would always bring everything to their Heavenly Father knowing that He cared for them so much. They were secure in God's love for them both. He was proud of her, for trusting in God for them all.

They bowed their heads and thanked God, who had brought

them both together and for bringing Tommy through this operation and for giving them both, the peace and the strength to get through it.

Holding onto God showed them, that God did indeed keep all of His promises. Holding on fast to God, gave them the strength they needed in every situation. For had God not said in His Word, *'I will never leave you or forsake you?'*

They had both known God was so near to them, even when they themselves were apart. God did indeed care for them, for He held on to them too!

Soon Tommy's health was restored again and he worked well on the farm. He was careful not to strain his new hip and he took things a little slower. He wasn't completely free from pain in his hip yet, and his other joints such as his hands and knees were sore at times, but he was so thankful to be able to work again and enjoy life on the farm once more.

Chapter 12. **Rachel**

Rachel was growing very quickly and followed her father around the yard as he looked after all the animals. She soon learnt the names of the animals and knew the difference between the cows, the horses, the chickens, the sheep and the other animals on the farm.

Her favourite animal was the family sheepdog who was called Roly. Rachel loved to go outside in the yard or into the garden to chase around with him. Roly was a good sheepdog and Peggy watched them playing together many times with such joy in her heart. She was pleased that Roly was so gentle and playful with her little girl. Roly knew Rachel's voice and as soon as he was let out of the shed each morning, he would go straight to the back door to see if Rachel was there to play with him, cheerfully waiting for her, wagging his tail and hoping for a treat!

Peggy loved her friends calling to see her and soon there was a group of them meeting each month on the farm for a time of fellowship and encouragement. While the mums all met together enjoying one another's company the little ones played with their toys and with each other. Rachel soon joined in with them making friends and there was much chuckling, noise and laughter going on! This time together became a time of strength for each one of her friends from the church. After everyone left, Rachel was always ready to go for a sleep!

Most of the young children would meet up at church and go into the Sunday school together to learn more about Jesus. As soon as they saw each other at church they would be so excited and run eagerly into the schoolroom to see what they would learn that day.

After church and Sunday school one particular Sunday, Rachel chatted away to her father about what she had learnt about Mr. Noah.

"Da, do you know that lots of animals went onto a big, big boat one day?" she said smilingly, "and do you know that there was two of every kind of animal on that boat as well? Do you think there would be two Rolys on that boat, Da?" she asked her Dad seriously.

Tommy laughed, "Of course Rachel. God would not forget about sheepdogs like Roly now would He?" he replied, tickling her.

"Do you think there would be two cows and two chickens as well on the boat?" she carried on excitedly.

Again Tommy laughed, "Yes, I think so. Two of everything means two of all kinds of animals Rachel; every kind of animal, even the cows and the chickens".

"Why did they have to go on a boat, Da? It must have been h-u-g…e… to fit them all in," she said, with her arms stretched out as wide as possible.

"Well Rachel, God told Mr. Noah to build a special boat called an ark, to save Mr. Noah and all his family. But God also saved all the animals from drowning as well. The way they could be saved was by going onto Mr. Noah's big boat," Tommy answered her, "so that saved them all from drowning in the big flood!"

"Do you think God will have to do that again and do you think that Roly would be saved in the new boat, Da?" Rachel enquired.

Again Tommy smiled to himself. "Rachel, do you remember that lovely bright rainbow that we saw in the sky a few days ago? Do you remember me telling you that God had just put it there, right then, when we looked up and saw it in the sky? God placed it in the sky for us to see all of its beauty, and," he declared, "it was also to remind us that God will never destroy the world like that ever again. No, Rachel, Roly will not have to go on a big boat like that to be saved."

"I love rainbows, Da, with all those pretty colours," she said, as she danced up and down with delight.

"Roly is safe here with us, Rachel. He is your special friend isn't he? He so looks forward to seeing you every day as he waits for you to come outside to play."

"I'm glad about that, Da. I don't want Roly to be put in a boat! I want to keep him here with me always. Yes, he is my special friend," she said as she ran away from her father, running up the hill with Roly chasing playfully around her feet!

Tommy and Peggy delighted in the fact that they could talk to Rachel about Bible stories, even if her imagination did run away with her at times and she got the facts muddled up. God would sort that out later on, he thought to himself quietly.

"Thank you Lord, for Rachel," he spoke out loud, "Keep her close to you."

Rachel grew up to know that when she prayed she was talking to God. She had heard her parents talk to Him lots of times, and she knew they loved Him so much. So she talked to God too. It was lovely to talk to God but she wondered to herself, "Why haven't I seen Him yet?"

"Da, Grandpa told me that God is everywhere. Why can't I see Him?" she asked one day, not long after the chat about Mr. Noah and the ark.

Tommy was unprepared for this question that day as his mind was on other things. However, he stopped and looked at Rachel. The look on her face was so enquiring. 'How do I answer this?' he thought to himself for a second.

"Well, come along here and sit by me, Rachel," he said to her. As she sat down she snuggled up close to him on the bench.

"You know that God is in heaven looking after us don't you Rachel? Do you remember Rev. Malcolm talking to us about heaven one day? Heaven is where grandpa Malachi is and it's where everyone who has ever loved God is, right now. Those who have already died before us are in heaven with Him. Well, God is there in heaven too along with His Son, Jesus."

Peggy and Tommy had already told her that Malachi had died a few years ago and that was why Grandma Tegan was on her own now, living with Patience at Keita just down the road from Gooseberry Farm. She liked to visit her grandma at Keita as often as she could.

"God is in our hearts when He lives inside us, do you remember that, Rachel?" she listened hard to him and nodded her head. Tommy continued, "When we go to church God is there as well. That is why we can praise Him and thank Him for loving us. Rachel, when you look at the mountains and the trees and the animals and the seas and look at all of God's nature around us, God is there also. We can't see Him with these eyes now but we can see how beautiful and how powerful He is, to make so many lovely things. God has made everything, so when we look at His creation we know that God is everywhere."

"So when I look at Roly I can see that God made him and God is clever," she said. At least she is getting the point, Tommy thought smiling to himself.

Rachel continued talking, "Da, if God made everything, that means He made me, so now He lives in my heart, because I have asked Him to. Will I see Him one day like I can see you?" she asked her father.

"Yes, Rachel. We will all see God one day. But only those who love Jesus will see Him in heaven. Now we can see Him in the beauty of creation and in the beauty of a flower. We can feel Him inside us in our hearts as well. This is a special kind of 'seeing', Rachel. It's 'seeing' by faith."

"Well I love Jesus, so I will see Him next week," she exclaimed. "I am going to see God, Da," she said confidently.

Rachel was so delighted. Now she could tell grandpa Carter that soon she would see God. She was glad that she loved Jesus. She would always love Jesus she thought as she ran off to play.

Chapter 13. **God's Secrets**

Rachel loved being outside with her father but she also loved helping her Mother too. On this particular day a few weeks later, she was helping her Ma to make some cakes for tea. As usual she was asking questions. Now it was Peggy's turn to answer them.

"Ma," she said,"I like the picture on the wall over there, the one with the big church and the path up to the front door. It's a really big church. It's a bit like our church in the village, Ma. Is God in that church too?" Rachel enquired.

Peggy glanced at the picture as she so often did when she worked busily in the kitchen. Every time Peggy raised her eyes or stopped to look at the picture, its meaning became more and more precious to her. This picture was hers and Tommy's. Their very own! It would be their guidance for all the days of their lives.

"Yes, God is in that church, Rachel. Churches are where people can go and meet with God. They are set apart especially for people to see God and know that He is there," she answered her daughter.

"Is that why those two people are walking up the path to go to church to see God, Ma?" she asked.

"That picture is of a young couple being joined together who are going to worship God in that church. Just like when you, your da and I all go to church every Sunday."

Rachel thought about it some more and went and stood in front of it looking up at the picture again.

"I like that church and I like our church. You like that church too, don't you Ma, because I see you looking at that picture lots of times? Can we go to that church one day, Ma?" she enquired.

"That picture is very special to your da and me, Rachel. It is particularly important to your da. There is some writing at the bottom of the picture which is a verse from the Bible and it is your father's favourite verse. Shall we read it out loud together?"

Peggy walked over to the picture and looked at it again with her young daughter.

It says, '*Seek ye first the kingdom of God and all these things shall be added unto you.*'

Rachel repeated the words after her mother and then added: "That's what Da says a lot isn't it Ma?"

"When we go to church or to any other church, we are doing what God is asking us to do, Rachel. God is saying, 'Put me first in your life and I will bless you'. It means that when we love God with all of our heart – that *we are* putting Him first. Then when we love everything else after that, God is pleased with us. Going to church means that God is our everything. We go to learn more about Jesus. You like learning about Jesus in Sunday school don't you, Rachel?" Peggy asked her.

"Jesus lives in my heart and I love going to church with you and my da. God is the very first, Ma, the very first in my heart," Rachel answered her mother.

"Rev. Malcolm tells us God loves us more than anyone else and I love God more than anyone else too. But I love you and da very first as well!" she continued excitedly. "Why are those birds in the picture, Ma?"

"Well, when you look at those words in the Bible, God tells us that He looks after the birds and He cares for them just like He cares for us. In fact God tells us that the birds are special to Him but we are even more special to Him than they are, Rachel. So we don't need to worry - God will look after us, always."

Peggy remembered again why this picture was so special to Tommy and her. Yes God will never forget them and He will bless them always. She was very grateful to God as she thought about that and said a quiet prayer in her heart.

Both of them went back to the table to continue making their cakes. Rachel was singing out loud, the chorus, '*Yes Jesus loves me. Yes Jesus loves me. Yes Jesus loves me. The Bible tells me so.*' Peggy joined her in the song, full of praise to the God whom they met in church every week; yes, in a church like that, but also whom they met in their home every day. She was so very glad about that for God was everywhere.

Later that day the cakes came in useful when Peggy and Tommy had unexpected visitors for tea! Everyone was told that Rachel had made the cakes. She was so happy. Grandpa Carter was especially happy and liked her cakes very much. She loved making her grandad happy. She jumped onto his knee and cuddled close to him.

She whispered in his ear, "Tomorrow, Grandpa, when we go to church, I am going to tell God that He is very first in my heart. Ma told me that God asks us to put Him first. Is God first in your life too, Grandpa?" she asked him.

"Yes sweetheart," he answered her laughing, "God is first. He is my very best friend too. God will be very happy when you tell Him that, I know."

"What are you two whispering about over there?" asked Tommy. "Come on let us in on the secret."

As usual in their home the evening ended with prayer and a Bible reading. Carter prayed for them all and they would tell God that He was first in all of their lives, and that they wanted to grow in their knowledge of Him every day.

A few weeks later when Peggy was collecting Rachel from school she tripped over and hurt herself. She didn't want Rachel to notice that she had tripped and fallen but Rachel could see that her Mother was a little upset.

"Why are you sad, Ma?" she asked her as she held onto her hand.

"Oh, it's nothing dear. I just feel under the weather a little that's all, but I will be all right when I have had a wee rest. Come on then, let's away home and make your da some tea. I expect you are hungry as well aren't you?" Peggy said, trying to keep her voice calm and normal.

Rachel soon forgot about her Mother being sad and started to lay the table for tea. Tommy came in from the yard and he sat in his usual chair. Rachel was chatting away to him, asking questions all of the time and with great excitement. She loved it when she had her parents all to herself!

After Rachel had gone to bed that evening, Peggy told Tommy about her day. She told him that she had fallen over earlier and that she was tripping up a lot lately. But it usually had happened when no one was around, but today she had tripped in front of Rachel and she had noticed it.

"Do you think it is something to worry about Tommy or am I just being over anxious?" she asked him.

Tommy was a little concerned but as he always did, he reassured her that it was just an accident and that she would be fine.

However, when they were praying together that evening he brought his request to the Lord.

"Lord God, you know that Peggy and I trust you for every

day and I ask that you will just come alongside Peggy and undertake for her in everything that she is concerned about. Lord, please help her today, and help her to keep trusting you. Thank you for your love for us and for your care. Amen."

During that night Tommy lay awake by her side and quietly prayed to God. He gently laid his hand upon her and put her in God's care. He also asked God to undertake for him too, because he felt that his other hip and knee were causing him some pain. He prayed to the Lord his God about everything, but he was not going to tell Peggy or anyone else anything just yet to cause them any unnecessary worry. He would just keep an eye on Peggy for himself and see that she was all right. "Help me God to trust you for our lives, for both of our lives. I know that you are with us. Take us day by day and watch over us, I pray. I praise you, Lord and I thank you for your faithfulness. Amen."

He concluded his prayer and then went to sleep, trusting all things to his heavenly Father.

The next day everyone got up out of bed as usual and God watched over this precious little family with His love and care. God knew his children. He poured out His spirit upon them for He knew what was going to happen in their lives in the near future. But He also knew that they would seek Him with all their hearts. For their future was safe in His care.

Chapter 14. **Under His Wings**

As the weeks passed by, Tommy knew that he would have to revisit the doctor again. He had tried to cope with the pain in his hip on the other side to the one that had previously been replaced, but was realising now that he possibly needed a replacement in his right hip too. That would be all right he thought, but it would mean extra time off work again. The farm needed to be seen to and he didn't want to put any more work onto his father. He knew Carter wouldn't mind at all but he liked to do things himself and his father had enough work to do.

He also realised that his dear Peggy was not herself at all. He had been watching her over the last few weeks even more closely and noticed that she was stumbling a little more and sometimes she accidentally dropped things if she was trying to do too much at once. He didn't want to see her struggle like this.

It upset him to see his Peggy becoming a little irritable at times and he knew she was beginning to worry about herself. She seemed to be forgetful and disorganised. This was not like his dear Peggy! She was always so ordered with her days planned out with precision. He must get himself better so that he could help Peggy even more and be there for her.

One morning he decided to make an appointment with his doctor. As the doctor examined around his hip and knee areas, he diagnosed that Tommy required another hip replacement. He sent Tommy for x rays and tests for rheumatoid arthritis. This seemed to be in all of his body and it confirmed to Tommy the reason for the pains and the discomfort that he was getting in his hands and joints.

The doctor explained to Tommy that the tests had revealed that Tommy did have full blown rheumatoid arthritis which was the cause of the pain and degeneration in this hip, back and knee joints. A few years had passed since he had had his first hip operation so that meant they could organise another one for him as soon as the hospital could arrange it. Before the year was out, Tommy would need another operation for a new knee replacement as well.

Dr. Wood was very sympathetic with his patient and tried to encourage Tommy that he had healed very well after the first operation where it didn't take too long for him to get up and about again.

It would all work out well for him and he would have some medication to help him through it all. Tommy would have much more movement after these operations but the doctor did warn him that the work on the farm may become too much for Tommy in the future so he should try and get some more help.

Tommy wanted to talk about Peggy to Dr. Wood but he thought that he would leave that until Peggy had seen him for herself. He would be with her then, to support her all the way and stand by her side.

He left the surgery that morning with a positive attitude though. At least he could have surgery and the pain would lessen again. There was hope for him. Then if Peggy needed surgery or anything he would be strong enough to help her through it.

As soon as he arrived home, he made a cup of tea and sat down and told Peggy about requiring surgery on his right hip, and then later on he would have a new knee put in as well.

"But it's all right, our Peg. I will soon be up and about after the op and get on with my jobs again. There is no need for you to worry about me, lass," he told her.

Peggy did worry though, "How will we manage Tommy? Will you ask Carter if he can help us with the work on the farm? I can manage some feeding and see to the chickens and do what I can," she told him.

"We will manage all right, Peg. Yes, my da will come and help us like he always does. Everything will work out just fine. I will see him tomorrow and explain things to him."

Later on that night Tommy and Peggy were at the Family Altar as usual and were reading from the Bible together, from 1 Peter chapter 5 and verse 7 where it says, *'Cast all your anxiety upon the Lord because He cares for you.'*

The reading went on to tell them to stand firm in their faith and to trust in God, who will Himself restore them and make them strong.

They bowed their heads together and held hands, thanking God for speaking yet again into their hearts.

"Thank you Lord," Tommy prayed,"for reminding us of the devil and how to resist him and stay strong in you. Thank you that we don't need to walk even one day on our own, but that you are always there to pick us up and restore us. We won't worry Lord. We will resist the worries that the devil would try to put on us and together we will keep close to you, trusting you to bring us through all these things. We have your word to us so we put you first in our thoughts and in our lives."

As the next few weeks went by, Tommy had a date for his operation and the Lord spoke again into their hearts, telling them to live close to him and He would be their refuge.

They read together from Psalm 91. *'He who dwells in the shelter of the Most High will rest in the shadow of the Almighty. I will say of the Lord He is my refuge and my fortress, my God in whom I trust.'*

Further on in the Psalm it continued, *'Because He loves me'* says the Lord, *'I will rescue him. I will protect him for he acknowledges my name. He will call upon me and I will answer him. I will be with him in trouble. I will deliver him and honour him. With long life will I satisfy him and show him my salvation.'*

With the promise from God that when they were living close to Him He would shelter them and be their refuge and strength, Tommy and Peggy felt great comfort and strength to walk the path planned out for them.

Tommy went into hospital. Carter and the others helped out on the farm. Evie and Tegan made sure that Peggy and Rachel were looked after and everything was taken care of.

Rachel enjoyed seeing her father come home again after the operation and Peggy watched as he 'rested in God' each day in his favourite chair by the Rayburn.

All their needs were met and every day Tommy and Peggy testified of God's care for them, telling their family and friends about their safe refuge and rock, who was God, and who had overshadowed them in and through all things. Indeed, they saw the scripture words come to pass in their own lives, that when putting God first in everything, He allowed them to see just how much He does keep His promises to all those who do trust Him completely.

Now they knew what it was to dwell close to God. They knew what it was to feel that refuge and fortress surrounding them. They knew that God cared for them even more than He cared for the birds of the air.

Many people came with gifts of food to bless them through this time of great difficulty. People from the church helped with lifts to the hospital and helped with looking after Rachel, so Peggy had no concerns about anything. She was amazed at how quickly time went by and how soon she had her Tommy home again.

Tommy gained strength every day and was soon taking short walks around the garden and in the yard outside. He stood outside in the fresh air and thanked God for His goodness towards his little family. He then prayed for God to undertake for Peggy. He had seen her quietly struggling with things and these did not go unnoticed by him. Peggy was the love of his life and now it was time to look after her and give her his all.

She was forgetting things even if they had only discussed them the night before. She was a little down at times and seemed almost as if there were the beginnings of depression coming upon her, but she would always be uplifted in their Family Altar times. These times were very special because even when Tommy became concerned for her, God helped them to give it all to Him and He helped them carry their load. Together with their Maker they were always willing to take one day at a time and so they were being strengthened.

Later on that day Rachel came home from school and was so pleased to be able to sit with her father and listen to him telling her more Bible stories. Tommy enjoyed these special times and was delighted that Rachel has such simple trust in God just as they did. It pleased Tommy that his home was such a happy home and he delighted in his Heavenly Father once more.

Life went on as normal for a few more months with Tommy gaining increasing strength and achieving small tasks. However, Tommy constantly watched his dear wife, noticing how she was struggling more and more with the ordinary daily tasks but was trying not to complain about anything. My, how he loved her! He did not think it was possible to love someone so much as he loved his Peggy.

They continued as a family to dwell in the shelter of their refuge and felt the overshadowing of God upon them, where they just felt safe and secure. It didn't matter what was happening in their lives. They were safe and secure from all alarm! God was their rock and fortress.

Chapter 15. **Peggy**

Peggy was so happy. She had the most wonderful husband and daughter that anyone could ever wish for. She loved her home and she loved how happy her family was. They were so blessed with having both her mother and her sister and Tommy's parents nearby for any support they might need.

She loved those monthly morning gatherings when her friends came to her home and they all talked about God and encouraged one another. Each month she looked forward to them arriving, so much so that she couldn't wait for Tuesdays to come around again. Tuesdays were her days! They were so special.

Peggy didn't realise how much of a strength she was to those around her who were watching her and standing in awe at what she told them. Neither did she realise how her face shone so clearly to them all, that her God, her Lord and her Saviour was her everything no matter what she went through. Yet for Peggy these special friends were her very own strength too and they were the ones that kept her going!

Her friends enjoyed going to the gathering at Gooseberry Farm each month, just as much as Peggy enjoyed them coming to her home. And this month was going to be no different.

Tuesday morning arrived and it was a lovely, crisp, sunny day when Peggy opened the kitchen door to let them into her home. Jenny, Mary, and Penny arrived early. These three friends lived in the village and Peggy had gone to school with them all and now they were married with their own children. All except for Penny that is, who was not yet married although she was going out with Archie. Archie was another friend who had attended the same school as them.

Later, Jane, Laura and Tess joined in the group and much laughter and encouragement filled the room.

Laura and Tess had recently joined their church and so they were new friends, but it didn't take long for them all to feel as if they had always known each other for years.

The group was growing in faith as they openly shared how God was blessing them and helping them in their individual families. Not one of the friends wanted to miss this special time together. They always had a closing prayer before they left and God sealed this time where He reached out to where they were and touched their lives in so many different ways. They always had stories about God's faithfulness and His love towards them, His children.

Peggy decided to make another drink, so she stood up to collect up the cups and saucers but accidentally knocked her leg against the table and fell to one side. She managed to straighten up a little, but seemed unable to pick up the cups. Jenny came to her aide and helped her to take them to the sink and wash and dry them. Peggy seemed disorientated but tried not to show it.

"Shall I make the drinks, Peg? I'd love to help," Jenny asked, as she turned to the others asking them what they would prefer to drink.

Mary noticed that her dear friend was getting uncomfortable so she went up to her and guided her back to her chair and sat her down. Mary sat next to her and Peggy began to relax a little.

The drinks were handed out and once more the conversation continued. They were all aware that their friend was struggling and had been struggling for a while, but no one wanted to embarrass her by bringing it up. Yet their love for her encouraged a safe place for Peggy to open up.

After a little while she was calm again and Peggy decided to confide in her friends. Now it was the right time she thought, to say what was happening to her. "Thank you, all of you, for being such special friends to me. I do so enjoy our times together. I have been delighted when we have shared our hearts at different times and how God has helped each one of us through so many things. But I want to share something with you now that I have been waiting to share with you - I have longed to have you all together to share this, because we are family.

I am struggling with my health. I have been trying to ignore the fact that I seem to find great difficulty at times to carry items and I seem to drop things and I have even fallen over in front of Rachel recently." She hesitated a little. "Tommy has noticed that I'm not well and we have spoken about it together, but I feel I need to talk about it and confront it now and get it out in the open. There doesn't seem to be any option as I don't seem to be getting any better."

Her friends just gave her time to speak, and waited…

Mary spoke up for the others at that moment when she saw Peggy didn't quite know how to continue. Mary and Peggy had been friends for many years.

"We love you Peg, and we are so glad that you are able to talk to us like this. We want to be of help to you. You always put us first and now it's time for us to help you. Have you been to the doctor about this? You know, you will feel so much better after talking about it, instead of worrying yourself about it and keeping it all bottled up."

"I just thought every day that things would get better and that I was being clumsy. Yes I think you are right, Mary. It is time for me to go to see Dr. Wood," she replied quietly.

Laura walked over to her friend, "Would you like me to see if Dr. Wood is free today, Peggy? I could take you in, if you like."

Jenny passed Peggy her drink and she sipped it gently. Peggy felt the love her friends had for her. She was so blessed. Tears began to well up in her eyes.

For something to do, Jenny stood up and started to tidy up a little in the room. Everyone else sat and listened to Peggy share more of what was troubling her. Peggy was glad to be able to voice her fears and yet she spoke of how God was her strength, her stay and her rock.

Nearing the end of their morning, Peggy was feeling better just knowing that she was not alone. She smiled at them all and continued, "Thank you, girls, for all your kindness and your love, and thank you for coming here this morning. Shall we ask God to take care of us all this month until we meet again? Does anyone want to say anything?"

Mary said, "I think we should pray for Peg now. Let's ask God to meet her need and to help her in this?"

They all bowed their heads and together they prayed for Peggy and for each of their own needs. They knew that God would never let them down. They thanked God for how He had brought Tommy through his last operation and for his healing and then they prayed that God would undertake for Peggy, their dear friend, when she would go to see the doctor.

They left the group knowing that they could not have done anything better than bring their friend to God in prayer; to their God, the One who knows all things and to the One who was in control of all of their lives.

After they left, Peggy felt the peace of God enter into her soul. She was so grateful that her life was in God's hands. She knew that without a doubt God would take care of her, whatever the outcome!

When Tommy came in later that day she told him about their morning together and how she had shared and talked with her friends telling them how she was feeling.

They decided together that the next day Tommy would take her to see Dr. Wood, but they would not tell Rachel anything yet. They didn't want to worry her until they had something definite to tell her.

Rachel came in from school that afternoon and everything was as normal in the Fearne household. They enjoyed an evening together talking about the farm, playing snakes and ladders, followed by their usual Family Altar time before Rachel went off to bed.

Again God reminded them that He cared for them so much and He would take care of them just like He cares for and notices the sparrows. When one of them fell to the ground, God knew all about it! Yet how much more did He care for them, His own dear children.

How this portion of scripture came to them time and time again, reassuring them of God's unfailing love.

Tommy walked the short walk with Rachel to school the next morning and then returned home to get the car and take Peggy to the surgery. Dr. Wood had told him that he was on the waiting list for a knee replacement and hoped it wouldn't be too long.

Then it was Peggy's turn to tell the doctor what had been troubling her for quite some time now. Dr. Wood listened intently with many thoughts going through his mind.

Tommy also relayed his thoughts to the doctor and they both felt as if they were unburdening themselves and were being listened to. Dr. Wood gave them time and did not rush them. After all, he knew them as friends now, after all these years of looking after their parents before them and throughout Tommy's illness. His heart was heavy for them. How much more would they have to suffer, he thought quietly to himself?

In a little while when he felt he could speak, Dr. Wood said he would take some tests along with some more blood tests. They would hear from him as soon as he had any results.

Life continued the same for them all for a little while. Tommy gained in strength and Rachel enjoyed helping her parents as much as she could. Peggy coped, but continued to struggle with everyday things.

Sunday arrived and the family went to church. Peggy met her friends there and they went into the service. Rev. Malcolm was on top form and preached an amazing sermon which gave each of them the strength to go through another week. They always left church uplifted and encouraged. God was very real and He spoke into their hearts, reminding them yet again that He was always with them. They met up with their friends and family there after the service and were delighted to see the church growing with new families and people joining them most weeks.

Tegan came to their home for Sunday dinner that day and Peggy told her mother that she had been to see the doctor. She had the strength to tell her what had been happening over the past few months and shared all her concerns with her.

Tegan, although upset, was pleased that Peggy had done something about it and had been to see Dr. Wood. She too had noticed Peggy wasn't quite herself recently, and was glad something was being done about it.

The rest of the day they enjoyed the beautiful sunshine by walking in the garden, and being out in the fresh air. Rachel enjoyed her grandmother being there and held her hand and took her to see the animals and collect the eggs.

"Come on, Grandmother Tegan. Let's go and collect the eggs and see the cows. Come on, Grandmother, come on," she said as she grabbed Tegan by the hands pulling her along in her excitement.

Tommy and Peggy laughed and went inside again to put the kettle on for tea, before Tegan would leave for home again, later on that evening.

The next day Peggy heard from Dr. Wood that he would like her to go to the surgery to see him, as he had got the test results back. Tommy accompanied her there and they entered the doctor's room when the buzzer rang.

"Good morning both. Do come in and take a seat," Dr. Wood said, as he beckoned them into his room showing them the empty chairs and inviting them to be seated. They both sat down very close to each other, holding hands.

"Welcome. How are you today Peggy?" he enquired gently.

"I am just the same doctor, thank you. Nothing has altered," Peggy answered with a smile.

"And do you have your appointment for your knee replacement yet Tommy?" he enquired of Tommy.

"Yes," Tommy replied, "the hospital has written for me to go in next month for my knee replacement. It will be about 18months since having my last hip done," Tommy replied.

Doctor Wood coughed and then he looked at Peggy, wishing with all his heart that he didn't have to say what he was going to tell her. "Well Peggy we have had the blood tests back. I would like to send you to the Neurological Department for some more tests. I need to be sure. I'm sorry to put you through this. I need to know some more details and along with your family history, I trust that I will find out what the problem is. It shouldn't take too long for this test to come through though. I will phone up for you now and make the appointment. Is that all right with you?" he asked her gently.

"Yes, thank you," Peggy answered hesitatingly.

"Good. I will do that for you now. I'm afraid that there is the possibility that you may be suffering from Huntington's disease. We have looked at some of your father's history which confirms to us that this was what Malachi was suffering from in his later years. We were unable to diagnose it then of course, but now with all the medical progress that we have made, we may be able to give you a proper diagnosis. I am sorry to have to tell you that this is a hereditary disease and it does pass down through the generations. I am so sorry Peggy."

Tommy looked at his darling wife and his heart sank. She looked stunned at the news but she graciously thanked the doctor for everything he was doing for her. She was shocked by all of this and remained silent.

"Thank you, Doctor," Tommy spoke for her, not knowing what else to say. "So what happens next?" he asked, on Peggy's behalf.

"We will see what the neurological tests reveal and then we can help with medication. I am afraid there is no cure for this disease but the medication will help slow down the symptoms and enable you to cope better. We will make you as comfortable as we possibly can. I will assure you of that," he said apologetically.

"Thank you doctor," was all Peggy could say at that moment.

Dr. Wood made the appointment for her and then they shook hands and Tommy and Peggy walked out of the doctor's room, stunned and shocked.

Dr. Wood lifted his heavy heart to the God, whom he knew would help them to bear this news. Where did their help come from? It came from the Maker of heaven and earth!!

When they arrived home, Tommy made a cup of tea and they sat quietly sipping their drinks, almost too afraid to speak. Peggy began to cry softly.

After a little while Tommy spoke gently to Peggy. "Peg, this is a shock for us and especially for you, my darling. It will take some time for it to sink in. Shall we just ask our loving Heavenly Father to help us right now, Peg?"

Peggy nodded her head in agreement, and Tommy quietly prayed to the Lord for strength, wisdom, and for guidance in all of this. He thanked God for being their refuge and for holding them in His arms just as His word says for times like this, *'Underneath are the everlasting arms.'*

God was their strong tower and they were running into it right now. It was the only safe place they knew.

Then they just sat there, Tommy holding her in his own arms and waiting for God to strengthen them both. They were assured of being in God's care and protection. Slowly God's peace pervaded their hearts and they received His strength; the strength to walk one day at a time, with Him by their side, for their future was very much in His hands.

Chapter 16. **A Few Years Later .....**

Ten years passed by and it was now 1970 and Tommy, Peggy and Rachel had known and felt God sustaining their family throughout everything that they had endured.

He who feeds the birds of the air, and He who cares for the flowers of the field and dresses them in their glory, was the same God who continually sustained them and gave them their strength.

Over the years, Rachel had grown into a beautiful young lady who cared and helped her parents and her grandparents in every way that she could, for they were her life. She was so full of love for all of her family and she enjoyed God's very real presence in her own experience. She had learnt so much from her own parents' example, that to put God first was the only way to live an honouring life before Him and before others so that God would be seen and glorified. She wanted everyone to know that her God was amazing and filled every part of her being.

Rachel was now in her teens and had many friends of her own in the church. She was popular with everyone and was a great help in the Sunday school and in the children's work. As she cared for people, everyone knew that she had inherited her caring nature from her parents and grandparents before her.

Because of all the suffering she had witnessed her parents go through, God had given Rachel a particular love and compassion for others, to help them. Rachel really was a servant of the Lord, living her young life by serving those around her.

Tommy and Peggy lived their life so that God would indeed receive all the glory. In all the sufferings which they both were going through, they always maintained such a sweet nature, holding no gripes or groans, either with God or with those that they loved.

Tommy cared for Peggy in such a loving way it made Rachel cry. Everyone could see just how much her father loved his wife. She was so proud of them both. And yet there were many times when her own heart felt like it would break as she watched them struggle through life on a daily basis.

Tommy had recovered from his knee replacement well enough, but as the years went by, he knew the real pain of the arthritis deep in his bones. This pain was so severe at times that he called out to God for relief. But he did not show any of this to his dear Peggy. Peggy was his life and he would not let her have anything more to worry about.

He was so proud of his Peggy. She had got used to the medication that she was on, so that her symptoms had slowed down a little. She managed to cope a little better, sometimes feeling less awkward, but on bad days she struggled to think and reason or even co-ordinate her limbs. She became so frustrated with herself then but yet she continued to thank God for His many blessings to her.

She had the love and care of her God. She had her Tommy whom she had known since they were little children and her Tommy knew her inside out. How she loved him. She thanked God for him every day. She thanked God for her daughter, Rachel and for her very evident faith in the Lord, which delighted her heart. Yes, Peggy counted her blessings, for they were many.

Peggy still enjoyed her circle of friends calling at the house especially now, as she was not always able to go out to church on Sundays quite as regularly as she had done before. She looked forward to Tuesdays very much for the encouragement she received from her group of friends. She still did not realise just how much God was using her to bless them as well, as they watched her remain strong in her faith.

Rev. Malcolm called regularly to see them and would help them in any way that he could. Sometimes he would pop up to the house to see Peggy, but if Tommy was out on the farm he would take a walk to find him for a chat. Tommy was always grateful for the support that the church and Rev. Malcolm gave to them. This was always such a blessing to them knowing that they were not alone at any time, but they belonged to God's family who were covering them in prayer and who were always ready to help them in any way.

On this particular day, Rev. Malcolm found Tommy sitting near the cow shed. He had just brought the cows in for milking and for feeding. He was waiting for them to feed a little more before he started on the milking. After putting out the hay for them and checking that the water troughs were full, Tommy decided to have a wee rest so he sat down for a few minutes.

His mind was on the farm. How the years had flown by. How he loved Gooseberry Farm. He was deep in thought, so much so that he did not notice the pastor approaching him. He continued thinking about the farm and all the work that it entailed. He then went to get up from sitting on the wall and enter the cowshed again to start the milking when he heard Rev. Malcolm call out to him.

"Good evening Tommy. How are you today? I have just been in to see dear Peggy. She is being looked after by that beautiful daughter of yours so I left them to come out and find you. I don't want to hold you up though," he nodded, as he noticed that Tommy had picked up the bucket to do the milking, "I will just say hello and see how you are getting on."

"Good evening Rev. Malcolm. It's good to see you here. The milking can wait a while," Tommy said as he put the bucket back down again onto the ground.

"Would you like to join me for a few minutes then?" He sat down again on the low wall, motioning to the Reverend to sit beside him.

"It's been a grand day today, Tommy. Have you managed to do all your work?" the pastor asked.

"Just the milking left to do and then shut up the chickens. Then I can go in and see how the women are doing inside. Thank you for calling to see us Reverend," Tommy replied, and then continued, "I am so grateful for Brett and Kyle who come along to help us out on the farm now. I'm not too good with this old arthritis that troubles me so much these days, but we do manage to get along and get the work done between us."

"How is Peggy getting on now? She always greets me with a smile but I can see the pain and frustration showing behind those eyes at times. How are things really Tommy?" the Reverend asked compassionately.

"Well actually, I was just contemplating things a little as you came along Reverend. I have been thinking about this farm and about our lives here. Things are not easy these days, but you know, we do have God's peace in our hearts. But it still hurts when I look at my Peggy who is in so much pain.

I get frustrated sometimes when I am not able to do things because of this arthritis that I have, but the faith that God has given us both, keeps us close to Him. Without God in our lives we would be in a very different place."

Tommy paused, cleared his throat and continued, "But now I am realising that I need to be inside with Peggy more, especially to help Rachel out, so I am wondering how much longer I can continue doing what I have always done on the farm. I find it difficult to bend and straighten up again. I am unable to carry bales of hay or lift things now in the way that I used to. I am depending more on Brett and Kyle. I think it's time to employ them both and do what I am able to do, as and when I can. I think I should probably become the manager of Gooseberry Farm and let them both run it and work it for me. I'm glad you have called today Reverend. I need some advice and help on this. What do you think?"

Rev. Malcolm had come to the same conclusion and was grateful for this opportunity to speak with Tommy.

"Actually, I have been praying for you Tommy. I have been praying for you to know guidance and direction for the future of Gooseberry Farm, so that you can slow down a little and spend more time with Peggy. I think that if you are able to let the lads go ahead with this idea then it is the right thing for you to do and it will take some pressure off you both. Brett is what, nineteen years old now? Well, he is a good worker and he can be trusted; that we know. He has his father to seek advice from as well and he will also help him when required. Kyle is just a few months younger, so they are both eager to do their best and make this work between them. Yes Tommy, it is time to make these changes."

He put his hand on Tommy's shoulder to show that he had confidence in what Tommy would do. After all, Rev. Malcolm thought, Tommy would not do anything without consulting his Maker and his Lord first, he knew that.

Both men prayed together and Rev. Malcolm left to go on his way. Tommy did the milking for the night. He settled the chickens in the shed, keeping them safe from the alarm of foxes or any other predators that might harm them.

Carrying the full milk can in his hands, Tommy said goodbye to the lads and went in to see how his girls were. After all, this was where he was at his happiest: inside the house with his Peggy and Rachel, feeling God overshadowing them all with His love, care and protection. Where else could he find this kind of comfort and strength, but in the love of His God?

Chapter 17. **Changes**

A little more time had gone by. Tommy had managed to free himself from much of the farm work to be with his dear Peggy. Brett and Kyle were showing great pleasure in working for Tommy, and the farm was in good hands.

From time to time Tommy would take a walk outside to look over things. The fresh air would do him good anyway. He stood leaning heavily on his stick, looking up towards heaven and thanked God for undertaking for them in everything.

Again Tommy was reminded of his verse, *'Seek ye first the kingdom of God and all these things shall be added unto you.'* God was watching over them. They had His care and His overshadowing always; all they had to do was stay under His wings.

He thought a little more. All this suffering, all this pain that he and Peggy were in, but Lord, I know that you know, and that you are always with us. Thank you. We can do this Lord, with your help.

He prayed in his mind a little more, "Please Lord, help Peggy. She is often anxious, worried and nervous - please give her your peace and bring her your healing. I trust you God, because you have never, ever failed us. In our pain we trust you."

Tommy entered the kitchen where Rachel had just helped her mother to get washed and dressed. They were both about to have a cup of tea.

"Would you like some tea, Da? Sit yourself down and it will be there in a minute," Rachel said lovingly. Tommy walked over to his chair by the Rayburn which was near his Peggy.

"How are you lass?" Tommy asked her gently, his heart full of love for her.

Rachel passed them both their drinks and helped her ma to drink slowly from the cup.

"My Tommy," she said slowly, "how are you? I am not able to relax my body enough today. I'm all jittery and nervous!"

Through all of this suffering, Peggy enjoyed just being with her Tommy. They sat quietly for a little while holding hands, as much as they could. Their love for each other was as evident now, as it was all those years ago when Peggy would run out into the farmyard to catch Tommy before he went home from working on the farm for her father. Many years ago now Tommy thought, almost twenty years now - but how I love her still!

Later on that night, the three people in Gooseberry Farm kitchen, snuggled around the Rayburn once again and turned to their heavenly Father. The Family Altar was never forgotten. Forgetting to pray to God would be like forgetting to breathe. It was so normal for them, things would be very wrong if this prayer time did not happen every day!

The reading that night was from Isaiah 41:10. Rachel read the scripture verses *'Do not fear, for I am with you. Do not be afraid, for I am your God; I will strengthen you. I will help you.'*

"Thank you Lord," Peggy prayed, "You know I am afraid. Thank you for your help." She cried a little.

Tommy put his arm around his wife and they thanked God for knowing just how they were all feeling and for speaking to them through this reading and reminding them that He would be their strength and for telling them not to be afraid. He was holding them close.

Life continued to be strained; yet they found all their strength in God. His words to them were true. As they held onto Him and trusted in Him, God was bringing them through.

Many times Peggy and Tommy just cried together quietly, but they were not without hope. Pain was very real to them both, so they knew how the other was suffering. But amazingly they knew the arms of God surrounding them as well.

Tommy was struggling with all the pain in his joints and recently his left leg had begun to weep. The sore would not get better, so when the nurse called in to see Peggy, he showed her his leg.

Unfortunately, this sore had turned into an ulcer. The nurse dressed it and then gave him some medication to help dry it up. For many weeks the nurse called every day to see to Peggy and to dress Tommy's leg ulcer.

At weekends they had someone else filling in for her. As the nurse cared for them both she could not help but see and feel their home to be different from the other homes she visited in her profession. She had been used to going into many homes, but this home she found herself looking forward to calling in to visit her patients there. She felt so sorry for this couple who were suffering with all of this sickness and had been suffering for many years before she had known them. Yet she loved being with them. They were different. It drew her to them. She wondered how they had such strength!

One day she had just finished her tasks a little early, having cleaned and dressed Tommy's leg and having helped Peggy with her own personal needs, she thought she would sit and have a cup of tea with them. She had already become good friends with Rachel, so Rachel had invited her along to church with her the following Sunday. She had been with her once or twice before, and she wanted to know more about this God - the God who was here in this home.

Hearing them all talking about their God and Lord, as their own personal friend and Saviour, made Helen want to receive this very same God into her own life. She wanted to know this God, who was now becoming very real to her. She wanted to experience having a faith like them. Helen then gave her life to God and became a Christian. Every visit of hers became a God-send into this home.

Helen was now like a member of this special family. They talked about God and they prayed together. They read the Bible each day and Peggy and Tommy found such joy with their new member of God's family. It was a joy to share Jesus with her. Helen prayed for this family every day. She prayed for God to help them and deliver them from their pain. Nevertheless, she could see that Peggy was getting worse.

Not long after this, Helen called at the home one morning to find Peggy still lying in bed, obviously in severe discomfort and pain. She took her temperature and saw that she had a fever. She was extremely unwell. Peggy was at significant risk of catching pneumonia. Peggy had lost a lot of weight and was finding it difficult to swallow or keep anything down.

Helen called in the doctor. Dr. Wood came as soon as he could and said to them that she had pneumonia and was very weak. He was very sad to see her so poorly. He left the room and found Tommy and told him that this pneumonia could easily take his Peggy's life.

Tommy knew in his heart that soon his dear, life-long best friend Peggy, was going to leave this world and go to a better place in heaven, where God had prepared His special place for her. A place where there would be no more pain or suffering; a place where she would see her Saviour, face to face. Knowing this, made his heart feel a bit easier, but how was he going to live without her - without his very own dear Peggy?

Tommy sat quietly by his wife's side holding her hand as much as he could. Her hands were rigid now, and his were bent up with arthritis, but they could touch each other and share their love for one another. Words weren't needed. Their love said it all!

That night Tommy and Rachel stayed up and sat by Peggy's bedside. Dr. Wood was there too. Peggy had lost consciousness and Dr. Wood gave her some more pain relief. She was not distressed anymore. Many prayers were spoken out loud and also silently in their own hearts by all of them.

When the time drew near for Peggy to make that great entrance into heaven, Dr. Wood quietly left the room and sat downstairs with Reverend Malcolm. Between them they lifted up this whole precious family to God.

A little while later Rachel came downstairs and told them that her mother had, "Gone to be with her Lord and Saviour." Rev. Malcolm held her close as she cried tears, tears of sadness but tears of relief also, for her mother was now free of all the pain and suffering of this life.

For Peggy, she was now with her God. She had gone to be with the One that she had loved all of her life and with the One who had watched over her and who had loved her too. She was running and jumping and now praising Him with all that she had.... She had been set free.... She was healed and in the presence of her Saviour forever.

Tommy sat awhile by Peggy's side. He wanted to be alone. He wept. He wanted to be quiet and feel her love for him again. He wanted to just love her still, by remaining there at her side for a short while longer. He knew that she would have known he had been there till the end. He knew she would have known that he would be praying for her through it all. He knew that. For he and Peggy had been one.

Now Peggy, his dear Peggy had gone to her reward. She was with the One they both loved with everything within them. He wanted to be there too. He would be there one day, with his Peggy again and see her sweet face once more!

He had to thank God for the knowledge that she was safe with Him. He would miss her. Oh how much he would miss her, but she was safe.

"Thank you God. I will see her again in Glory, when we shall both see you face to face and worship you together," he silently prayed. He wept again, but not without hope! He felt God speak deep into His heart those precious words which they had both lived their lives by:

'Seek ye first the kingdom of God and all these things shall be added unto you.'

Yes, he knew God had added to him again, even in this great sadness. He was not mourning without hope. He had the assurance, the assurance that Peggy was safe. He knew and had the peace that she was with God, and was not in pain anymore. He knew. Yes, he knew deep in his heart that he was going to see her again, one day!

God was adding to him even now, giving him His great peace and His comfort in his heart, just when he needed Him. Thank you, God.

Chapter 18. **Tommy and Rachel**

Now it was just Tommy and his little girl. Although Rachel was now a young lady of sixteen years, she would always be Tommy's little girl. Tommy was so thankful to have Rachel in his life now that his dear Peggy was no longer there to share it with him. He counted his blessings every day that Rachel was so much like her mother, with her kindness and all her help to him. She also brought young life into their home, with her strong faith in God, just like his dear Peggy had all down the years. He was so thankful to have her there.

Helen continued to come to the home to dress Tommy's ulcer, and he looked forward to her coming. They would have little chats about Peggy most days, and Helen would listen to Tommy as he spoke so lovingly about his late wife.

How lovely it would be to have been married to your best friend for twenty years and to have been able to have shared Jesus together, she thought. Then quietly she prayed, "Lord, will you give me someone to love like that; someone who will share my faith and share my life with me; someone like dear Tommy, Lord. Thank you Lord. I do delight in you, for your word tells me that, *'you will give me the desires of my heart, as I put my trust in you.'*

For Tommy it felt as if Peggy and he had never been apart as he remembered days when they were young children running into Sunday school and then times throughout their marriage doing things together, always one with the other. He felt as if he had lost one half of himself when Peggy died, but he was so grateful for the happy years they had shared. He held on fast to the One who he knew carried him and held onto him too.

Rachel, Tommy and Helen continued to go to church on Sundays. It was good to be together to worship God. When they met up after the service for a cup of tea, the whole congregation encouraged one another. Various people looked out for Tommy to see if they could help him in any way that they could. Some of the men were good at visiting Tommy and offering him help on the farm whenever he needed them. Others just called to visit him and to keep him in fellowship with his church family.

On many days after his breakfast, Tommy would walk out into the farmyard and see what was happening outside. Both the lads were a great help to him and he delighted in their hard work and their obvious care for the animals and for the running of the day–to-day things on the farm. He was pleased with them and he often told them so. He was a good boss to work for. In return, they both worked hard so that Tommy did not have to worry about anything. He enjoyed the times when they came into the house to discuss what was next on the calendar to do, regarding harvesting the crops in summer, or planting the seeds in spring, or deciding what to take to market to sell on market days.

The garden produce was successful and everything seemed to be flourishing. The farm was running well. Tommy lifted up his heart in thanks to his God.

"Lord, you have blessed me with these lads and I pray that they will know your blessing on their own lives. Thank you for taking care of the farm for me and for giving me this security in these times. As I trust you, you are adding to my life yet again, in keeping your word to me, that you will provide for all my needs when I put you first."

One day, many months later, Tommy sat in the kitchen at Gooseberry Farm, looking at the picture on the kitchen wall that still meant so much to him. His eyes filled with tears as he remembered all the wonderful times that he and his dear Peggy had shared the truths of this verse together and how much these words had lifted them and encouraged them to know that God, their God, was in control of their lives. But my, how he missed his dear Peggy! He still missed her so much! He thought of the many times they sat together and looked at this picture, both of them hearing the voice of God in their individual hearts, reassuring them of His constant care and provision for them.

But this day as he continued to look at the picture throughout the whole of that morning, the truth of those words couldn't and wouldn't leave his thoughts. It was consuming him. He looked again at it. Then he was drawn to the text written at the bottom of the picture. He read it out loud again marvelling at how many times God had spoken to him from that very same verse.

He continued to let his thoughts drift over his soul once more and then God seemed to draw his attention to the birds of the air as they flew above in the clear blue sky. Today, this whole verse came alive in his spirit. This God, His God, who so cared for the sparrows and fed them daily, cared for him and for Rachel too. His Lord, who looked after them and who always met their every need, was the same God who still had many plans for their lives today. His God, this God, who watches the sparrows and even knows when one would be injured and fall to the ground, really cared for him. He really did care!

His thoughts ran over and over in his mind even more, as he continued to meditate on this verse. Then God‘s peace came and filled his heart.

God knows about the birds of the air for they belong to Him and He is their Creator. He knows all about them, because He is the One who sustains them and keeps them. He is the One who sustains all of His creation, especially his children, even today. How majestic is His power! His thoughts ran on….

Tommy gently bowed his head and acknowledged His heavenly Father's care and sustenance for each new day. In his prayer he silently wept as he quietly prayed, "Lord, you keep me. I thank you for sustaining me through every day. I know that I am being kept by your love. I do trust you for all things and in all things. For you know when I sit and when I rise. Lord, you know all things that concern me. Thank you Lord.

Thank you for reminding me that the sparrows are in your care every day and that I am in your care right now. For your eye is on the sparrows - and as you watch over them, I know you are watching over me in the same way."

He felt God's presence surrounding him like an enveloping cloud.

That night, Rachel and Tommy read again the precious verses from Matthew chapter 6. They would never tire of reading this passage of scripture. God reminded them that He would see that they would never want for anything, because they were putting Him first in their lives. They were living for Him each day no matter what they were going through. Rachel turned to her father and together they remembered that day when she said to him, "Da, God is first in my life, very first!"

They enjoyed sharing these happy memories of earlier years, when Rachel was young in the faith. Tommy was so thankful for his little girl, all over again.

Rachel loved her father and she was a wonderful homemaker

as she helped and cared for him. She cared for the home by making it as comfortable and welcoming for them both and for those who called to see them regularly.

She was pleased to have the constant help of the lads on the farm as she watched how much her father appreciated them. She was grateful of his trust in the faithfulness of God. She knew he had this faith because he had known God throughout his whole life and he knew that God would never let them go.

Many nights Helen would stay over in the spare room with them at Gooseberry Farm enjoying their love and friendship.

Her faith was growing stronger and stronger. She wanted her faith to grow in God and she was experiencing new things every day. Yes, God was just as real to Helen as he was to both Tommy and Rachel. How blessed she felt.

Chapter 19. **Faith Shining Through....**

Three times a week Helen continued to visit Tommy to clean and dress his ulcer, but his leg didn't seem to dry up at all or improve in any way. She advised Tommy to rest it and put it up, but it seemed as if the ulcer was not going to heal for a long while yet. Helen wondered if Tommy would gain by having some respite in the local cottage hospital. She knew he would appreciate having all his needs taken care of by the nurses. Maybe this ulcer would heal with the constant care and rest. She would see what she could do for him.

The next week Helen organised two weeks respite for Tommy where she would be able to pop in to see him and see that he was being looked after.

So when Helen arrived at Gooseberry Farm as usual the next day, to clean and dress his ulcer, she told Tommy about the respite in the cottage hospital that she was arranging for him. Trying to encourage him to take time out and have a rest, she helped him to see that it would give Rachel a break as well.

Rachel thought that this was just what her father needed and told him so. Tommy agreed to go in for two weeks rest and care. Maybe a change and a rest would do him good, he thought to himself. And yes, maybe Rachel could do with a break herself and be free to come and go as she wished.

"Yes Da. I do think the rest will do you good. I will miss you so much but maybe this is the time for you to have a change and recuperate a little. You don't have to concern yourself about home or the farm, so take time to have a rest and enjoy the break," said Rachel trying to encourage her father to take up this chance of being cared for.

Helen confirmed the plans with them. It was arranged for Tommy to go into Madison Cottage Hospital for two weeks. Rachel could visit her father as and when she wanted.

The ambulance picked Tommy up early in the morning a couple of days later and when Tommy arrived at the hospital he was in good spirits. Rachel would be calling in that evening to see him and if he had settled in. It wouldn't be long until he would see her again. He knew that everything at home would be in good hands, so Tommy arrived with a deep peace in his heart.

Tommy soon made friends with everyone. He enjoyed

talking and chatting with the other patients and even enjoyed having some physiotherapy and other treatments that helped him with his arthritis. Every day the nurses dressed the ulcer on his leg and took care of all his needs, also helping him to shower and dress.

Tommy's faith shone out to everyone in the hospital. He never complained and always looked on the bright side of life.

He got to know some of the men and shared with them about his many happy years with his Peggy. Rachel came in to visit along with Helen and Tommy's strength was being renewed. His heart was filled with joy as he shared very simply, his trust in his God, to those who would listen.

Unfortunately, Tommy's knee was giving him a lot of pain and he was struggling to walk. With his painful knee and an ulcer on the other leg, Tommy needed a pair of crutches to help him get around the ward and with the short walk to the dining room. Sometimes he even had to use the wheelchair to do the greater distances.

In the middle of the week Tommy's doctor came and recommended that he have a new knee replacement on his left knee. This would be the second knee operation for Tommy. Over the previous years he had already had both his hips replaced as well as his right knee. So he agreed with the doctor after talking to Rachel, to have this new knee joint. He appreciated that he would find it more difficult and longer to recover this time as he was that much older, but he knew that he would recover given time. The date for the operation was soon organised for him with all the necessary arrangements made so that it would be done as quickly as possible.

Dr. Wood visited Tommy and reassured him that this would bring him some more release from the pain he was in right now and help to strengthen him with his walking.

In the meanwhile, Tommy's hands were so painful that he found it hard to use his crutches, but he never complained and just got on with it, knowing God's peace in his heart - the peace of knowing that God knew all things.

The respite was good for Tommy and the nurses arranged that after the new knee replacement operation, he would return to the cottage hospital respite centre for a few more weeks' recovery and get the extra help he needed.

Rachel took her father home and cared for him until the date came for his next operation.

The lads remained stable and trustworthy and again the farm was taken care of. Tommy had no worries and trusted his God to guide them all through this time.

These two months of waiting to go in for his operation went by very quickly and Tommy went into hospital to have his knee replacement. Everything went well and Tommy became stronger each day. He remained in the hospital for two more weeks and then went into the respite care for an additional few weeks, being encouraged to exercise it as much as he could. His knee was quite stiff but it did improve slowly and he was freed from much of the pain of the arthritis.

The ulcer on his other leg was still weeping. The nurses kept a large dressing on it to keep it clean and free from infection. Tommy had to have his leg up for most of the time to help the ulcer heal, in between all the physiotherapy and other treatments he was having. Tommy made good progress though, and he would soon be home again!

In all of this, Tommy's testimony shone through. He never complained of his lot or moaned about the pain. The nurses loved Tommy. He was a wonderful patient to look after. Everyone would miss him when he left to return home again. The atmosphere in the ward around Tommy changed when he was there with his very contagious, thankful spirit. A lot of the complaining seemed to stop as they watched this gentle man accept all the help he was given, so graciously.

After a few more weeks of care, Rachel brought her father home again and she made a wonderful nurse, caring for him in her own special way. She loved her father so much that nothing was too much trouble for her.

Helen continued to visit and dress his leg and would often call around after work to share a meal with Tommy and Rachel who were more like her own family now.

After some months Tommy was back to his normal self and could get out into the garden for a short walk often standing outside the farm house just breathing the fresh air into his lungs. He was so thankful to be mobile again, even if he was much slower now, and he always needed to walk with the crutches.

Many of his friends came to visit him and he was thrilled to talk about his faith with them. He was also strengthened by the love and care of those around him.

Chapter 20. **More Adversity**

Tommy noticed one day that Rachel was quiet; particularly quiet! He watched her and he saw that something was troubling her. He didn't say anything to her but as was his usual habit he prayed for his daughter. He did this for a little while longer and then one day he noticed something that brought fear and alarm into his heart. Rachel was beginning to show signs that concerned him. No! He wouldn't even think that way. What was he thinking! Rachel was fine. He would trust in his God to answer his prayers for her. Maybe she was just a little overtired, he reasoned with himself!

Sometime later, during their evening Family Altar time, Rachel picked up the Bible off the shelf to read it, but as she did so, she dropped it on to the floor. Struggling to pick it back up again Tommy's heart felt a flutter! He stayed silent for a minute. But he knew that this was the right time to speak to Rachel about his concerns for her. However, Rachel turned towards him first, her precious father, and with such concern on her face, she said slowly and gently to him,

"Da I have been struggling with picking things up for a little while now and I am struggling with getting some things organised in my mind as well. I see myself like Ma, doing things, or trying to do things, and then not being able to accomplish any of them. I haven't wanted to say anything to worry you Da, or cause you any concern. But I need you, Da. I don't want to cope with this on my own. I need your strength too."

She looked at her father with such sad eyes that his heart was filled with pain.

"What shall I do, Da?" she pleaded with him.

Tommy reached out his hands towards her, and held her own wee hand. It wasn't that comfortable for him to do this, but he denied his own pain. He held his beautiful daughter's hand and began to cry a little. Silently, the tears fell down his face. They cried quietly together for a wee while longer. This was a healing time bringing them together so that neither of them felt alone in any of this. But it was a time they had both tried to put off, not wanting to face any more struggles in this life.

They cried with each other, but also cried before their loving heavenly Father. Yes, He knew! God knew! He did know how they felt there and then. He knew that their hearts were breaking. After all, He knew them better than they knew themselves. They felt His presence surrounding them, pouring His strength into the deep parts of their beings at that very moment.

"Rachel, we still hold onto God, sweetheart. We both love Him with everything that is within us. He knows Rachel. He knows! Let's just ask Him to help us. We will ask Him to help you, and to bring you healing in this."

The thoughts and words that had come into their minds about all of this they did not voice out loud. They were too stunned to do so. They didn't need to voice their fears at all. For their God knew! God was there for them in the midst of all their struggles!

Tommy held his daughter in his arms now and together as one, they prayed to their Heavenly Father.

"Lord, I don't know what to say, but please undertake for my lovely Rachel. We don't understand this Lord, but we trust you. We trust you to help us, to heal us to hold us and to meet us with your grace. Help us Lord. Our lives are in your hands. We ask for your healing."

After prayer they sat for a little while longer in quietness, while God surrounded them and wiped their tears away by completely filling them with His presence. God knew! Yes, God knew! He would never let them go! They were both safe with Him.

Chapter 21 **A Very Present Help in Time of Trouble...**

Tommy and Rachel went to see Dr. Wood who knew as soon as Rachel started to share her difficulties with him, knew in his heart what she was going to say to him. He just sat and listened quietly. As he did so his eyes began to fill up. He listened to her tell him of the symptoms that were affecting her movements and her ability to hold things. He listened and prayed in his heart for them both. How much more could they take God, he said inwardly? How much more could anyone take?

Dr. Wood had been their doctor since before Rachel was born, so he knew the family well and knew all about their lives. He also knew their faith and their complete trust in God, so he gently and quietly lifted them up to God in prayer. Only God could bring them that comfort that they were going to need in the future.

Dr. Wood sent Rachel to the hospital for some tests that he knew were certain to confirm his greatest fear. He tried to comfort them as best he could. He reassured them that he would help them in every way possible to get all the help and support they needed.

Tommy took his Rachel home. Helen had kindly driven them to the hospital that day so she settled them into their chairs and made a hot drink of tea for them both. She served it in their favourite bone china cups. Then she quietly left them to be on their own. She knew God would come to them and hold them. They would not be alone.

After she left their home, she telephoned the minister and told him the sad news.

Straightaway Rev. Malcolm knew that God's word would be the only comfort that Tommy and Rachel needed at this moment.

His thoughts were guided to Psalm 46 which reads like this - *'God is our refuge and strength, a very present help in time of trouble. Therefore we will not fear, though the earth gives away and the mountains fall into the heart of the sea ..... God is within her..... Be still and know that I am God. God is God.'*

This psalm was the psalm that brought an answer to Rev. Malcolm's prayer for them when he called to see them. God *was 'their refuge'* and He was *'their help and comfort'* at this time. *Yes, the earth had given way underneath them. Their feet were no longer steady and sure.* At this moment they were beginning to fear what was ahead of them.

However, they turned to their rock and refuge for help. What else could they do? Where else would they go? God was the only One that would bring them through this and be there for them and undertake for them.

They listened to the words from God again and stilled their hearts before Him, longing to know God in the stillness. "God, please be God in our lives and in all of this," they prayed through their tears.

Rev. Malcolm quietly slipped out of the room and left them to receive all that God would give them there and then.

A visit to see Dr. Wood two weeks later brought the confirmation to them that Rachel did have the same illness that her mother Peggy had been suffering from. All of the tests showed that Rachel had inherited the disease from her mother.

Dr. Wood told them that Huntington's disease is unfortunately passed down through either of the parents, the mother or the father, to any children born to them. Any child has a fifty percent chance of getting this disease which is hereditary. The disease doesn't skip any generation. This usually reveals itself in adults about the age of 30 but can be earlier in some cases.

These early symptoms were what Rachel was already seeing in her body. Her movements were becoming more uncontrolled. She was becoming unsteady on her feet and she had a slight tremor.

Because of these things already happening, Dr. Wood prescribed her medication to help slow down the process and make it more bearable for her.

He looked at the family history of Malachi her grandfather and Peggy, her mother, suffering from this same disease, which had become all too real for them once again.

Tommy's worst fears were being realised as he watched and listened and heard Dr. Wood explain to them these things in a clear and concise way that would help them to come to terms with this and try to help them understand a little more.

"We will do all we can to make life bearable for you and make you as comfortable as we can. There are things that will help you with your symptoms, Rachel. Of course your faith will be a great comfort to you I know. We are always here to help you Rachel," Dr Wood said compassionately.

Tommy thanked the doctor and then took his beloved daughter home again to the sanctuary of their home.

Chapter 22. **Learning to Hold on……**

Tommy and Rachel sat quietly and peacefully in their home, thinking over all that Dr. Wood had told them about the disease. They now knew that this was what Peggy and her father Malachi had been suffering from. It was going to take a long time for this all to sink in with them.

As they sat there, they relived all that they had seen Peggy suffer through the years and now Tommy thought he was going to have to see his daughter go through the same things. His heart was heavy within him.

They were both going to need God's grace and His strength to go through all of this but God would be there for them, of this he was convinced.

Then God came in such an amazing way and poured in His strength, His grace and His love into them that they felt totally surrounded by His presence and they nestled into His everlasting arms once more.

Rachel silently held onto her faith in the God who would never let her go. All she needed to do was to hold onto Him and hold on she would!

A while later Helen called to see them. When she walked into the kitchen she immediately felt the warm presence of the Lord in the room. She felt His nearness but could also see on their faces and in their eyes that something was wrong.

"Hello Helen," Tommy greeted her warmly, "Do come in and join us. We have been to see Dr. Wood today. The news is not good, lass, I'm afraid. Sit yourself down," he said, as he invited her to sit in one of the comfortable chairs beside him.

"Rachel what is it?" she asked her as she went up to be close to her friend.

"Well we now know that Ma and grandad Malachi were both suffering with the same disease. Dr. Wood has confirmed it to us today and now I have the same disease as well. It is Huntington's disease, Helen. This disease is hereditary and passes down through the generations. I have this gene which has been passed onto me. Dr. Wood has given me some medication to help me. I feel that by the strength that God is imparting to me right now," Rachel cried a little more, "that I can be like my Ma and try to have a good testimony and bring God glory in this somehow. Ma always held onto her faith and I will do the same. Holding on is such a big thing of trust and I trust my life into God's hands," she continued, "but I am shocked that this is what I have. But God is my help in time of need. And oh how I need Him!"

Tommy decided to ask all the family over that evening to tell them the sad news.

Carter and Evie were the first to arrive and Evie helped to make the drinks as the others were still gathering. They sat down together while Tommy unfolded all that they had been told that day in the doctor's surgery. He relayed all the news of the history of the family and now his dear Rachel's illness. They were all stunned by this devastating news.

Tegan began to cry and went across to where Rachel was sitting and put her arms around her gently. How could this be she thought to herself? How could this be happening? Poor Malachi. How he had suffered. How Peggy had suffered and now Rachel as well. Please God help us, she prayed silently.

Patience sat quietly thinking it through. She realised that she would need to have some tests to see if she had the same gene for Huntington's disease. But surely she would have known by now if she were ill! How can this be happening to them?

Edward came to her side and held her close. No more words could be said.

That evening they comforted each other and everyone reached out to the Lord and held onto His great love for them. He who had been faithful up till now would continue to remain faithful through all of this. He was their strength and their stay whatever the outcome!

Later as everyone went to their own homes they stayed in the safest place of security they knew – close to the God who would not let them go…….

Chapter 23. **Shining Through, Yet Again!**

A few months later Helen moved into the family home at Gooseberry Farm with Tommy and Rachel. She became the full time carer for Rachel and for Tommy. Throughout all the heartache, they were to remain strong for each other.

How wonderful to know that God had saved her friend and now she was there to be their live-in carer, thought Rachel.

"Thank you Lord, for your faithfulness," breathed Rachel from deep within. "Thank you for bringing Helen into your family Lord and into our lives. Thank you for adding this blessing to us. Thank you for your care." Her heart was grateful!

Rachel was also very thankful to her God when she heard the news that Patience who had had the many tests for Huntington's disease was found to be clear of having the gene, so she was healthy. How they praised God for this miracle! Patience and Edward could now go ahead and plan their future and be happy with no fear of this sickness coming upon her.

Patience ran into the room to hug Rachel with tears streaming down her face.

"We will be here to help you though Rachel, to help and support you in all of this. Edward and I love you and will help take care of you.

We are hoping to live in Madison as Edward has just accepted another teaching post in Madison Primary. His time in Maxwell school has come to an end and this new post will be a new challenge for him. Our lives together have been planned by God and I thank Him for leading us this way and for bringing us together. How He has answered our prayers Rachel. God is so good!"

With Helen now living in Gooseberry Farm, Rachel and Helen grew together in their faith and Tommy rejoiced in his heart as he saw how Rachel benefited from their friendship. Yes, and sometimes he would hear a little laugh coming from the corner of the room, as Helen would tell and read the wonderful truths of the Bible to Rachel. Then they would try and guess where the portions of scripture were from as they read them out loud to each other. They found that in God's presence there was indeed fullness of joy, despite all the pain that surrounded them.

Knowing a great peace in her heart, Rachel remembered how

her mother Peggy had been victorious in her faith and had won through to the end, with her faith being very much intact.

She was grateful to have her father there with her and for the many times they talked about their life on the farm and of all the funny stories of what the animals had got up to and what she had done when she was a little girl. They talked of how she had loved to paddle in the brook taking a picnic along with her, as well as taking her many friends too. How she enjoyed listening to all the Bible stories of people like Noah, or Moses, or about Samson and many other Old Testament characters. She remembered times of running up to the Sunday school and playing with the neighbours' children along the way. She had lots of good memories as she also thought of all the love and guidance that her parents had always shown her and taught her.

At other times there were periods of heartache and sorrow when thinking of all the suffering that she was going through and what they were all enduring. She thought of times when she watched her father trying not to show her his worry and his concern for her, by putting on such a brave face. She thought of times when she watched him struggling with his own suffering, as well as coming to terms with her illness and yet still not complaining to anyone. She thought of times when frustration and awkwardness would overtake her and when she felt so awful and clumsy. These times were so hard, so hard, but she was not alone. She was never alone.

Then there were the times when she and Tommy would sit together in the kitchen and gaze at the picture on the wall, remembering the many occasions when they had put God first and when He had shown them His faithfulness to them, over and over, and over again.

This particular day Tommy turned to the portion of scripture in Matthew chapter 6 and read those familiar words again. He read about the flowers of the field. God said, '*See how the flowers of the field grow. They do not toil or spin - yet I tell you, they are robed in splendour'*. That is how much God cares for them.

"God robes the flowers of the field and He robes you and me Rachel, and you Helen," Tommy said looking at them both in turn. "He makes them more glorious and more beautiful, as they let Him clothe them in His splendour. Let us allow God to clothe us with His beauty so that we will shine and bring Him glory always. Let the brightness of His light show on our countenances and let it be seen in our speech so that our faith will shine out in brilliance and Hope. This is how we can be '*flowers*' in our home, by being full of the fragrance of Jesus."

Then they prayed together, "Lord, we thank you for filling us with hope and joy so that your splendour shines through us. Help us to be ever faithful to you. Thank you for adding to our lives your very presence and for clothing us with your beauty, to keep us trusting and holding on to you, so that your glory may shine through us, to others."

Chapter 24. **Sharing the Fragrance of Jesus**

Tommy, Rachel and Helen continued to share the fragrance of Jesus with everyone they met. Friends and family marvelled at their strong faith which they witnessed whenever they were in their presence.

In all their suffering they robed themselves with the robes that God had given them to bear all things they had to go through so they would bring Him glory. Gooseberry Farm was such a peaceful place to be. Everyone who came couldn't help but be touched by the power of God, who could keep and uphold His dear children by His faithfulness to them.

As the years continued to go by, this home was looked upon as a light upon a hill in the village of Maxwell. This family held onto God and His sweetness filled the place.

Times of blessing were a great strength to each of them. They had many good stories to tell of the loved ones who helped and kept this family together. Their strength came from those they loved and from the God who loved them. He gave them hope and joy amidst all the suffering, reminding them that in His presence – there is fullness of joy – and His joy would take them through.

The wedding of Patience and Edward had been so beautiful with the whole day full of happiness. They were married in Maxwell Church by Rev. Malcolm who just made it complete. Surrounded by all their friends and family from Sunday school days and other friends from the church the day was a great day of celebration. Edward had some friends from the school there and Archie, who was now married to Penny, was their best man. Tommy, Rachel and Helen counted their many blessings as they witnessed God's blessing on this happy couple.

Helen had met a nice young man called Graeme in the church who was a Christian and who loved to serve others. Helen had spoken so much to him about all the love she had received and seen in the Fearne family, beginning with Tommy and Peggy when she had first met them. She told him about their love for each other and how she had come to faith through the way this family lived. They had never preached to her but they had just lived the love of God in front of her.

And now Helen had found this wonderful person who would

share her life with her. How blessed she was.

As she shared all this with Graeme one evening her thoughts took her back to that day long ago when she had prayed that quick silent prayer, "Lord, let me have someone to love and to share my life with, someone like Tommy!"

God had heard her prayer and had indeed blessed her life with Graeme. How great was her God?

Tegan so loved living in her cottage at 28, Church Road. The cottage lived up to its name and the Lord blessed Tegan with many callers. Tegan and Edward had worked so hard in the garden and now she enjoyed opening up the garden in the summer months for people to call in for afternoon tea and a walk around. She served them many of the cakes which she and Evie enjoyed baking in the mornings at Beech Farm.

During their opening times Tegan was able to provide the 'enclosed place' for people to hear about the love of God as they strolled around the garden looking at all the shrubs and flowers so wonderfully displayed before them. She even put some labels on some of the plants that are mentioned in different Bible verses, or where they had been used for healing purposes.

Tegan's home, 'Keita' was a quiet welcoming place for those God chose to send and find solace and hope for their busy lives.

As Tegan herself got older, she and Evie enjoyed the peace of the garden as they communed with God, both of them knowing that God was receiving pleasure from their time spent with Him as well.

Carter and Evie were now getting older. Carter had recently celebrated his 70th birthday with a party at Beech Farm. Tommy and Rachel were delighted to be back at the farm. They watched as they saw Carter and Evie continue to be strong in health and in their enjoyment of each other. Tommy watched his parents some more. They were unaware that he was looking at them. He noticed them holding hands and delighting in all their visitors. He was so proud of them both. He couldn't quite take it in though, that his father was now seventy years old. Where had all those years gone to? Really, Carter had always looked the same to him but now he suddenly realised his father was not getting any younger. He was so grateful for all that his father had shown him down through the years and for all he was still doing for them.

As he lovingly watched his parents that evening he thanked God for them and for their strong faith which had reached out to everyone they knew. Carter and Evie were the most gracious people he knew!

Rachel in turn was watching her father in the same way with similar thoughts running through her mind. How privileged she felt, to belong to such a wonderful family. Her dad Tommy was the best father in the whole world. 'I love you,' Da she thought to herself. 'I am so very proud of you. You always put others first and your trust in God is amazing!'

Carter and Evie continued to enjoy all the celebrations that evening and for the rest of their lives they lived for God's glory.

They continually sought God for their son and their grand-daughter, Rachel, who needed to know the love and sustenance each day of the One who knew how to care for them, so much better than they ever could. After all He cares for the birds of the air, doesn't He? And He clothes the lilies of the field!

Chapter 25. **God's Provision.**

As time went by, Rachel became more rigid and her movements became far worse. It was very hard for her, as she tried her best to attempt things, but every task had become something major for her now.

She became a danger to herself and to those around her. These days she did not go far from the home at all. In fact, she hardly ever left the safety of the farmhouse. Dr. Wood called to see her often and to check on Tommy too.

Helen carefully looked after all of Rachel's needs and remained a firm friend and nurse, bringing Rachel through many difficult times. When it all got too much for Rachel, they both sat and cried out to God to draw near to them and to give them the spiritual strength they needed.

Although Rachel did not understand why this was happening, or understand how she could ever get through this, she never ever let go of her faith. She knew that God was the only One who remained the same in her experience. He was always the same, steadfast and sure and faithful. When she needed to be held, God came and held her close.

These days, no one could hold her close anymore, because all her movements were very unpredictable. Helen was amazing with her but Tommy was not able to come near to her, in case she accidentally knocked him over by her sudden jerks. How she felt for him and how she so missed his nearness. Yet he was near to her in his heart, and she felt his love for her every day.

Patience and Edward called in most days or as often as they could, to help and give Helen and Tommy some much needed breaks.

The doctor called to see how Tommy was getting on one day, when his heart felt heavy with concern for them both for now they were his friends. Tommy's arthritis was getting worse and his hands were not improving; in fact they were very inflamed and painful. As Dr. Wood summed up the situation in the home, he could see all the possible dangers ahead of them both and he worried how he would tell Tommy what was on his mind.

How was he going to tell Tommy this? Yet he knew he would have to do it soon for both his and Rachel's protection.

"How are you managing with those crutches these days,

Tommy? Are you able to grip the crutches safely?" he asked Tommy gently.

"Well doctor, I manage if I walk slowly and take my time. It is not easy, but I can get around. The thing I find hard is that I am not able to get close to Rachel anymore. She may swing out her arms and knock me over. She constantly drops things on the floor and I could so easily trip over them. I have to speak to her from a distance, sometimes sitting at the other side of the room. It is so hard for us both, but we do thank God that we have each other and we have Helen here helping us. God does look after us. We will manage, doctor."

Dr. Wood hesitated. "Tommy, I need to say something to you. I have a suggestion to make. It's not easy for me to say this, but it must be said. I want you to let me speak what is on my mind, and then I will leave you tonight and let you think over what I have said. Do not make a decision tonight. I will come back to see you in a couple of days for your answer.

As you have told me yourself, Rachel is now unpredictable with her movements and mood swings. These often cause her to be irritable which in turn cause more difficulties for you all in your home life. Being near her with the chance of an accident happening at any time is highly likely. It would cause you great damage if you fell.

I want you to seriously think about moving out into a new home that will be in sheltered accommodation where you will be watched over carefully, Tommy and where you will be safe from all harm. You cannot put yourself in this danger of falling over and harming yourself. Your arthritis is debilitating enough in itself. You do not need any more broken hips or joints.

Tommy, I know that you and Rachel are close but that relationship doesn't need to change. Nevertheless, the important thing is that neither of you will be hurt nor injured by anything that may happen here. Promise me Tommy, that you will think about this. Pray about it and allow God to still your heart. I am going now and will see you in a couple of days for your answer. God bless you Tommy. I will pray for you both. Goodbye."

Doctor Wood left Gooseberry Farm with a heavy heart but lifted up his burden to God who would, he knew, comfort and help Tommy and Rachel through all of this.

Tommy was broken hearted. He was shocked, yet when he

thought about it, it seemed as if this was the only answer for them. But how could he leave his dear Rachel? How could he leave this dear farm of his? He would not speak of this yet with Rachel. No he could not: not today. It would be impossible!

He went into his room and cried out to God in prayer. He didn't know how to put it into words the deep heaviness that was within him, but his God knew his heart and his thoughts. He let his sigh be his prayer. God would hear him, of that he was sure. It was too hard to speak. There were no words! But God knew!

Silently the tears fell down his cheeks and he bowed his head and waited on the Lord, who came gently to him wrapping His arms around Tommy. "I know!" Tommy heard God say, "I know!"

That night Tommy had difficulty sleeping, not because he didn't trust God, but that he already knew in his heart that this was the only thing he could do to alleviate the problem of any further accident happening, either to him or to Rachel. But how could he not see his Rachel every day? He spoke to God asking for His help to get him get through this.

"Lord, help us all to come to terms with this. Help Rachel, Lord. Help her to know I am not leaving her, that I will still be her da and I will not be far away."

Then he laid his head on the pillow and the Lord came and gave His beloved, sleep. God was very present to Tommy, His child, in the time of his trouble; yes, very present indeed.

Chapter 26. **His Ways Are Not Our Ways.**

The next morning when Tommy awoke he felt as if he was still in a bad dream. Everything that had happened the day before came flooding back into his mind like a flood at first! But then he remembered that the Lord had drawn near to him and had given him peace. He was not going to fight this. It was the only safe option that he and Rachel had for their protection.

He managed to get himself up out of bed and walked through into the kitchen using his crutches. He saw that Helen had already seen to Rachel and had her sitting at the table for breakfast. Taking his chair and sitting down with them he greeted the girls,

"Morning, girls. It's breakfast time again. Shall we say grace then?" Tommy said, as he bowed his head and prayed a blessing on the food set before them. Then he prayed for God's blessing on what this day was going to hold for each of them.

"Morning, Da," Rachel answered him. "What are you planning to do today? Is grandpa Carter coming to see us today?"

"Well," says Tommy, "When we have all finished eating our breakfast I have something I would like us to discuss together. It is quite important," Tommy said looking gently at them in turn.

Helen continued to serve them both making nice hot tea and toast for Tommy served with some of Evie's homemade blackberry jam. Rachel enjoyed some hot porridge with some fresh fruit to sweeten it a little, followed by a hot cup of tea. When they had finished their meal, Tommy told them of his visit from the doctor the day before. He outlined all that Dr. Wood had proposed and then he waited a while for it all to sink into their minds.

"But Da, why? Why does this have to happen to us? We will be all right here if we just take it slowly Da. Does this really have to happen? Are you really having to move out of Gooseberry Farm and leave us here, Da? There has to be another way for us. There just has to be?" Rachel cried out despairingly.

Rachel could not quite comprehend what all this would mean for them. Helen went across to her and waited quietly by her side as she shed a few more tears. Helen and Tommy cried too. This was all too much for them. Again they waited for this to register in their minds. Was there another answer to their problem?

But God came and poured in His divine strength and

understanding into each of their hearts at the same time. They felt His peace pervade them so that each of them knew without a doubt that this was God's provision and protection for them all. This was the only way. Now all they had to do was ask God to go before them on this new path and bring them His help and strength for this part of their journey.

Dr. Wood came back a few days later as he had promised Tommy. He spent some time talking things through with each of them. Helen was a wonderful help and support to Rachel. She promised her that she would always be there for her, to care for her as long as she was needed. She told her that it was a joy to be her friend and be able to stay at Gooseberry Farm and look after her.

Later that day Tommy called his father Carter over to discuss the running of Gooseberry Farm with him. Carter and Evie gave Tommy their blessing on the new plans and entrusted their son to the God who would take care of his every need.

They decided together that Tommy would continue to own the farm for as long as Rachel and Helen needed to live there. He would be speaking with Brett and Kyle to ask them both to manage and run the farm for him as they had been doing for the past few years. They were very capable workmen and God had blessed their work for Tommy.

Tommy would set up some plans for when the day would come when he would need to sell the farm in the future. He decided that Brett and Kyle would have the first opportunity of buying the farm for themselves, should they want it.

Tommy knew that God would bring them through all of these decisions because he had brought it all to the Lord in prayer as was his usual custom. God was first in all of his planning.

Rachel, still a little teary, spoke quietly with her father.

"Da, I love you so much. I will miss you greatly. Why does this have to happen to us, Da? We have been through so much already? Yet I know it makes sense for both of us to keep us from any harm. Oh Da!" she cried.

Tommy who was very near to tears himself tried to comfort his 'little girl' but he could not find the right words, yet spoke gently to her.

"Darling Rachel," he said full of compassion and love for her. "Darling, this seems the only way for us and if that is right then it must be God's way. For we have asked Him to guide us in our decisions. Now we must trust Him.

I love you so much Rachel. It breaks my heart to have to leave you here but I do know that you will be safe here in Gooseberry Farm. You have Helen, Brett and Kyle to help you. But most of all, God is here to take care of you. He never leaves us or forsakes us. He will give you His peace."

Quietly Tommy bowed his head in prayer. This was his natural response to everything that came his way. He cast all his cares on the One who cared for them all.

"Lord God we entrust ourselves to you now. We leave all these decisions in your hands and we leave the farm in your care. Thank you for sending us Helen and for giving to us Brett and Kyle. Bless them all Lord. And thank you for providing us a 'way out' from more harm and for giving us 'a safe place' to live in. Thank you for your provision."

That day God gave this precious family and all those that surrounded them His everlasting peace and hope; hope that in the new things and in the new ways that were set before them, God would continue to show just how much He really did care for the Fearne family.

Chapter 27. **Very First !**

Rachel and Helen watched as dear Tommy left for his new home. The day had arrived all too quickly. They were all broken hearted, but oh how they felt God surrounding them and holding them. Helen helped Tommy get his things together and organised everything for his comfort in his small home about a mile or so away from Gooseberry Farm. Helen would not be his nurse now, but he would be taken care of by the wardens on duty in the complex. This included the nurse belonging to the surgery who would be calling in to see him every other day. His ulcer was improving and was healing slowly so that was one positive thing for him.

Tommy's new home had a lovely compact kitchen, a front lounge, a bedroom and a bathroom. All the rooms were fitted out for people with disabilities and Tommy would have his own carers coming in every morning and evening to help him get up and be put to bed again each evening.

Tommy had wanted to leave his picture on the wall at the farmhouse but Rachel had insisted that he took it with him. It had been his and Peggy's picture. Tommy had it put up on the wall in his lounge where he could see it every day. This picture and the scripture on it was his rock and he would always have many sweet memories as he looked upon it; sweet memories of Peggy and himself and then later on, of his Rachel and all of his friends having the many discussions about seeking God first in their lives.

Tommy moved in to his new home but he was never alone. The God who had been with him at Beech Farm and in Gooseberry Farm, in his and Peggy's home, was now with him in this place. And he did feel His God so very near to him, always.

When Tommy had said goodbye to Rachel and Helen he prayed that they would always know God's presence there, as God had indeed always dwelt in that farmhouse ever since he could remember.

God was very present when Malachi his father-in-law and Tegan his mother-in-law owned the farm all those years ago. God had continued to dwell there all through his and Peggy's married life, so Tommy knew God would always be there for his Rachel for God had promised to never leave his children alone.

Helen called in to see Tommy that evening after he had

moved into his new home. She saw that his heart was heavy. Tommy was pleasant, but there was something missing inside him. She knew it was his own very dear Rachel that he was missing. She prayed with Tommy. She promised him that she would visit him again the next morning and left him with some good wholesome food for his supper.

Tommy slowly made his way to his bedroom that evening. The carer popped in to help him undress and then when she saw that he was safe and tucked up in bed, she left him with a hot drink on the bedside table. She would be in again at 8.30am the following morning to help get him up again.

Tommy picked up his Bible and turned to Matthew Chapter 6. Where else would he turn to on the very first evening in his new home?

He read the familiar words which warmed his heart and he heard God speak into his soul again, those precious words,

'Do not worry about your life..... I care for the birds, how much more do I care for you.... Do not worry! Your Heavenly Father knows what you need.'

God's peace came into his heart and he felt the Lord surround him. He knew he was not alone. He prayed for Rachel and for Helen and thanked God yet again for Helen who was also like a daughter to him. He laid his head to rest and the Lord sent his guardian angels to protect him and give him peace.

When Tommy opened his eyes the next morning, he was a little disorientated at first but then it all came back to him. He was not in Gooseberry Farm anymore but now in his new home. It took a little while for it to register in his mind, but then he remembered the day before and everything that had taken place. He turned his heart straight to the Lord and thanked him for a peaceful and restful sleep.

Later on that morning, Tommy picked up the telephone to speak with his precious daughter. Helen answered the phone and then switched it on to loud speaker so that Rachel and Tommy could have a chat together.

"Hello Rachel. Good morning sweetheart. How are you today? How are you feeling my darling?" Tommy spoke with a little tremor in his voice but trying not to show it.

Rachel cried a little at first. She couldn't help it, but she also had God's joy in her heart. She had longed to hear her father's voice, and it sounded as if he was right there in the same room with her.

"Da, Da! It's so wonderful to hear you. I'm all right Da. How are you? Do you like your new home? Did you sleep well? Is your home nice and cosy for you?" She wanted to know everything about him all at once!

Tommy's heart felt a flutter! Yes! He and Rachel would talk like this every day. In fact every morning and every evening they would talk on the telephone. This was wonderful. They would always stay close to each other and once a week he would be able to go and visit her on the farm. He felt a little more hopeful. His heart lifted inside him with a fresh new vision of the way ahead. God would continue to bless them always.

"Rachel. Yes, I am fine and I have slept all night. God is with me, and I have His peace in my heart because He is taking care of you too," Tommy answered her cheerfully.

"Da, I did ask God to look after you and I asked Him to be with us as well. God is still here. I feel Him in this room, Da. I know that He will never leave me or forsake me and I thanked God for Helen, Da. We will be reading the Bible together as well every day, Da. We will!" said Rachel, "and I will see you on Thursday, Da."

Thursday was only four days away. Tommy's heart lifted again. Yes Lord, all will be well, he thought. I will see my dear Rachel soon.

"Rachel, we will be able to read the Bible together over the phone you know, and we can still keep our Family Altar times. Would you like that Rachel?" Tommy asked her cheerfully.

"Da, that is so amazing. Thank you Da. I would love that," she answered him quietly.

"Hey Rachel, do you remember that day when you gave your life to God? Do you remember that you said that you would seek first the kingdom of God, and then God said to you that all the other things that you need, He would add to your life? Do you remember Rachel?" Tommy asked her.

"Yes Da, of course I remember. I was only little then but God heard me and you were with me weren't you Da? God is my everything and I hold onto Him, to help me and to take care of me all the days of my life. He will speak to me won't He, Da?" she enquired of him.

Tommy laughed, "Yes, Rachel, when you put God first, He

will *always* help you and *be there* for you and *be with you.* But always remember to put God first, Rachel?"

"Yes, Da. I do. God is Very First!" she answered him.

Tommy gave a deep laugh. The laugh came from deep within him. All was well. Yes, all was well. A huge peace settled in his heart. God came to Tommy that day in a fresh new way.

"Yes, Rachel, very first. Very first indeed!" he said.